THE THING'S MOUTH WAS BLOODY!

Joey swallowed hard and made himself look out the window again. The thing—whatever it was—had stopped moving.

It couldn't be a black plastic garbage bag. And it didn't look like a dog, either. It was too short and squat to be a dog. Joey shivered as he watched the rain wash down the sides of its slimy body. So what was it?

"Um, Molly. Come here," he said, trying to keep his voice from giving away his fear. She was smart. Maybe she could figure out what it was.

Molly had started digging things out of her dilapidated grocery bag and lining them up on a desk. So far there was a box of crackers, a jar of peanut butter, and a box of breakfast bars.

She gave Joey a frightened look. "What for? Not if it's about that thing out there. I don't want to look anymore."

"I want to ask you something. Come on," he urged.

Suddenly the thing turned a shadowy face toward the window. Joey gasped and shrank against the wall. Its mouth *was* bloody! Its eyes were gleaming, and it was looking straight at him!

Read these BONE CHILLERS **from HarperPaperbacks:**

BONE CHILLERS

TEACHER CREATURE

BETSY HAYNES

HarperPaperbacks
A Division of HarperCollins*Publishers*

This is a work of fiction. The characters, incidents, and dialogues are products of the author's imagination and are not to be construed as real. Any resemblance to actual events or persons, living or dead, is entirely coincidental.

HarperPaperbacks   *A Division of* HarperCollins*Publishers*
10 East 53rd Street, New York, N.Y. 10022

Copyright © 1995 by Betsy Haynes and
Daniel Weiss Associates, Inc.

Cover art copyright © 1995 Daniel Weiss Associates, Inc.

All rights reserved. No part of this book may be used or reproduced in any manner whatsoever without written permission of the publisher, except in the case of brief quotations embodied in critical articles and reviews. For information address Daniel Weiss Associates, Inc., 33 West 17th Street, New York, New York 10011.

First printing: September 1995

Printed in the United States of America

HarperPaperbacks and colophon are trademarks of
HarperCollins*Publishers*

❖10 9 8 7 6 5 4 3 2 1

For my friend, Danny LoCicero,
in New Lenox, Illinois

TEACHER CREATURE

Chapter

"**P**sst! Hey, Dolinsky," Joey Powers whispered loudly. Nate Dolinsky, who sat at the desk across the aisle, was his exact opposite in looks, but they were best friends anyway. Nate was short and chubby with sandy blond hair, while Joey had brown hair and was as skinny as a pencil.

Nate shot him a quick grin. "What do you want?"

"Bet you're afraid of old man Johnson's dog," said Joey.

"No way!" said Nate, looking insulted.

Joey grinned wickedly. "I climbed into his pen yesterday. Bet you're too chicken."

"Boys!" shouted Mr. Vernon, the sixth-grade

1

teacher. He was tall and skinny, with a pinched face and a long, bumpy nose, and he was standing in front of a map of the world and glaring at the two boys. "Stop your talking this instant! We're having a very important lesson about a hurricane heading our way. You'd better listen *closely*, so you'll know what to do when it gets here."

Molly Murphy, the class brain who sat in front of Joey, flipped her dark hair over her shoulder as she turned around and peered at him through huge glasses. "Don't listen, Joey," she muttered. "That's okay. Maybe we'll get lucky, and you'll blow away!"

"Molly, that pertains to you, too," warned Mr. Vernon.

Joey snickered and sank down behind Molly so that Mr. Vernon couldn't see what he was doing. Then he opened his notebook and began drawing a huge black dog with a studded collar and blood dripping from his razor-sharp fangs, which he planned to pass to Nate as soon as Mr. Vernon turned back to his map.

Of course old man Johnson's dog didn't look nearly that mean, but it didn't matter. It was part of the game he and Nate played, daring each other to do things to see who was the bravest.

2

Maybe he could talk Nate into climbing into the dog's pen on the way home from school.

"I want all eyes this way, please. Yours, too, Joey," Mr. Vernon barked.

Sounds just like old man Johnson's dog, Joey thought, but he sat up straight and looked at Mr. Vernon.

"According to the advisory message issued by the National Hurricane Center just a few minutes ago at noon, a large tropical storm named Hurricane Leslie, with winds of 112 miles per hour, is heading toward Florida and could make landfall here at the edge of the Everglades in Ochopee sometime tonight."

Joey sat up a little straighter. He had been a little kid when Hurricane Andrew had hit Florida a few years ago, mowing down trees and churning up the swamp just outside their town, but he could remember some things. Like how disappointed he had been when his parents had grabbed him, piled a bunch of stuff in the car, and run like scared chickens to a motel somewhere up north in Florida.

He had heard that when the storm hit, it had blown toads out of the swamp, and they had fallen all over town like rain and in some places had even piled up two feet deep. And alligators

3

had roamed the streets, and snakes had come up into peoples' houses through the bathroom plumbing. But he had missed all the fun. He hoped his parents wouldn't evacuate if Hurricane Leslie hit Ochopee. He wanted to be here to see it this time.

Sighing, he tuned in to Mr. Vernon again. He was pointing at the map as he talked.

"As you children know, hurricanes are circular wind storms, like giant tornadoes, that are born off the coast of Africa. Their winds carry tiny particles of sand from the Sahara Desert that mingle with teensy dust mites from the flat savannas of Africa."

Joey perked up. It was hard to imagine that the wind that might blow into town tonight had come all the way from Africa.

Cool! he thought.

"They tumble and swirl across the vast heaving waves of the Atlantic Ocean, sucking up droplets of salt water, tiny pieces of plankton, and other microscopic forms of sea life from the dark ocean, while the storm grows bigger and stronger"—he scraped his pointer dramatically across the map—"until it reaches here. The Gulf of Mexico." He stabbed his pointer at a spot in the Gulf not far offshore from Ochopee.

4

"Hurricane Leslie is now at latitude 25.2 degrees, longitude 83.6 degrees, and moving toward us at thirty miles per hour."

Molly's hand shot into the air. "Let me mark it on the tracking map, Mr. Vernon! Oh, please?" she begged. "I know right where to put the X."

The teacher smiled benevolently at her. "Certainly, Molly. Come right on up. I'm glad *someone* has been paying attention to the lesson."

Molly jumped up, threw Joey a look of superiority, and pranced to the front of the room. She picked up a black marker and wrote an X on a spot near the Florida coast.

Joey's scalp tingled as he stared at the map. It didn't look very far away.

"Now, boys and girls," Mr. Vernon continued, "you will be officially dismissed in five minutes."

The classroom went up for grabs. Kids were jumping up and down and screaming for joy.

Nate socked Joey on the arm. "Want to see me jump into old man Johnson's dog pen?"

"Boys and girls, you aren't listening!" shouted Mr. Vernon. "No one leaves this room until I've finished."

Everyone quieted down immediately.

"That's better," said the teacher. "Now, I want all of you to hurry home and help your parents get ready for the storm. You know what to do. Collect canned goods and bottled water to take with you when you evacuate. Board up the windows and doors. Bring in the lawn furniture and anything else that might blow around. And boys and girls," he said, holding up a finger dramatically, "above all, *stay safe!* I want to see all of you back here in the classroom after the storm."

"Suuuure, Mr. Vernon," Joey muttered sarcastically as the dismissal bell rang and kids poured out the door. "We're all just *dying* to see you back in the classroom after the storm, too."

Nate came up behind him as he started down the sidewalk.

"Hey, it's sure getting windy," he said, looking around at the palm trees. They were tossing their fronds around as if they were angrily shaking their heads. "Do you think Hurricane Leslie's really coming?"

Joey had also noticed that the wind was picking up. And there was a funny smell in the air. Like something was blowing in. He remembered how his grandfather used to sniff the air. He could always smell it when a storm was coming.

Maybe I'm like him, thought Joey, looking around warily. The sun was still shining, but there was a funny glow to the sky. It made his pulse race. Something was definitely brewing.

"Still want to tease old man Johnson's dog?" asked Nate.

"Naw, I've got a better idea," said Joey. He raised one eyebrow and shot a questioning look at Nate. "Unless you're chicken."

"You're the one who's chicken," said Nate. "I can outdo you any day of the week. And I can do it with my eyes closed, my legs cut off, and my arms tied behind my back. Try me."

"Okay," Joey said excitedly. "Listen up. Let's sneak home, pack up some survival stuff, and come back to school. Everybody will be gone by then, and we can ride out the storm right here—*all by ourselves!* Then we'll find out who's chicken, if we don't blow away first."

Nate's mouth dropped open. His eyes widened, and a grin spread across his face.

"You're on!" he shouted, and the two boys ran off toward home.

Chapter

2

Joey's parents worked, but they both were home when he got there. His father was on a stepladder on the front porch, nailing sheets of plywood over the living room windows.

Joey found his mother in the kitchen, frantically slapping peanut butter-and-jelly sandwiches together and keeping an eye on the TV, where the weatherman was giving the latest storm forecast.

"This is an advisory from the National Hurricane Center in Coral Gables, Florida," the man on the screen announced. *"Hurricane Leslie is growing in intensity and is now located at latitude 25.8 degrees, longitude 81.9 degrees, and is moving toward the west coast of Florida at twenty miles per hour."*

"Oh, Joey. Thank goodness you're home," she said. She swept a strand of hair off her forehead, streaking her face with purple goo at the same time. "The storm's getting closer, and we're going to evacuate! We've got to hurry before they close the only road out of town!"

She stuffed the sandwiches into a cooler and headed out of the kitchen, murmuring, "Oh, dear. I forgot the flashlights."

Stopping in the doorway, she turned back to Joey, giving him a dazed look as if she'd just remembered he was there. "Honey, go get your sleeping bag and your toothbrush and pack a few clothes. We don't have a lot of room in the car, so don't bring very much. George!" she called to his father as she hurried away. "Did you remember to buy batteries?"

Joey trotted down the hall to his room. This was going to be easier than he thought. With total confusion all around him, he could gather his stuff and sneak out without being missed for ages.

A few minutes later he was hurrying to meet Nate. He had grabbed some peanut butter-and-jelly sandwiches and containers of orange juice out of the cooler and stuffed everything into his backpack. Now he braced against the wind, clutching his sleeping bag in front of him and fighting to keep it from acting like a sail and pushing him backward.

Nate was waiting on the corner a block from his house.

"I brought my boom box," Nate shouted, but his words were almost lost in the roar of the wind. "I got some candles, too, in case our batteries run down. And chocolate chip cookies."

Joey grinned at his chubby friend. "What more do we need? Let's go."

As they headed toward school, a police car was crawling through the streets, its loudspeaker blaring. "ATTENTION ALL CITIZENS OF OCHOPEE. THIS IS AN ORDER TO EVACUATE! I REPEAT: EVERYONE MUST EVACUATE. HURRICANE LESLIE IS HEADING THIS WAY. EVACUATE *NOW*!"

Rain was pelting them as they made their way through town. A few stores were still open, and they were crowded with people getting last-minute supplies. In the street, cars loaded down with families, pets, and belongings were streaming along the lone road out of Ochopee and heading through the swamp toward the Interstate.

"Maybe we should get some candy bars in case we run out of food!" Nate shouted as they passed Colombo's Food Mart.

"I didn't bring any money," said Joey. "Did you?"

Nate shook his head.

Just then Colombo's door opened, and Molly Murphy hurried out, carrying a bag of groceries. She stopped in her tracks when she saw Joey and Nate, and her mouth opened wide.

"Where do you think you're going?" she demanded. "Don't you know there's a hurricane coming? You should be heading home instead of in the opposite direction."

"None of your business," growled Nate.

"And why are you carrying sleeping bags? You guys are up to something, aren't you?" Molly narrowed her eyes and glared at them.

Ignoring her, Joey leaned into the wind and headed on down the street. Nate hitched up his sleeping bag and followed.

Molly ran after them, lugging her bag of groceries. "I'm telling!" she shouted. "I'm going straight to your parents if you don't turn around and go home right now."

"Drop dead!" yelled Joey. He hated Molly Murphy more than any girl he knew. So what if

11

she was the smartest girl in school? She was always sticking her nose where it didn't belong!

When they reached the school, Joey stuffed his sleeping bag between his knees so it wouldn't blow away and tried the front door.

It was locked.

"You must be stupider than you look if you think you can get into a locked school. Boy, do you ever deserve the trouble you're going to get into," Molly scolded. "Just wait!"

The wind was howling in the rafters now. Joey retrieved his sleeping bag and fought against the gusts as he and Nate moved to the back door. It was locked, too.

Molly gave them a triumphant smile.

Suddenly he had an idea.

"Hey, Nate. Let's try the windows in our classroom. Mr. Vernon had them open today because it was so hot. Everybody left in a hurry. Maybe he forgot to lock them."

"Gotcha!" yelled Nate, and the boys tore around the side of the school.

Molly was struggling with her bag of groceries as she followed. The rain had made the paper soggy, and the sack was splitting. She cradled it in her arms like a baby and hurried after them.

The second window Joey tried slid open

easily. He tossed his sleeping bag and backpack in first and tried to boost himself up over the sill, but a big blast of wind broadsided him, knocking him to the ground.

"Hurry! It's getting worse!" Nate shouted over the roar of the storm.

Joey struggled to his feet and made it through the window on the second try. Barely. The wet sill was slick, but he slithered across it and landed on the other side with a loud thud.

"Here, Nate! Throw in your stuff and then give me your hand," he shouted.

He huffed and puffed and finally tugged Nate into the room.

Suddenly the sky opened up. Torrents of rain crashed down, driven by huge gusts of wind that bent the palm trees flat on the ground. Lightning jackhammered through the clouds, and thunder shook the building.

"What about *me!*" screamed Molly. She was clutching her soggy grocery bag and staring up at them through terror-filled eyes. Her dark brown hair was plastered to her head. Her glasses were speckled with raindrops. Her jeans and T-shirt clung to her body.

"You better run home before you—" Joey shouted, and then stopped. She looked so pathetic standing there with the storm swirling around her. And what if she couldn't make it home? "Come on!" he yelled, and thrust his arm out the window. "And hurry up! We don't have all day!"

A few minutes later the three of them stood together in the classroom, staring out the window.

A shivery feeling passed through Joey as the wind howled outside and rain pelted the glass. The hurricane was coming. *Soon.* They had no choice now. They were all alone in the school until the storm passed.

"I'm scared!" wailed Molly.

"Not me," said Nate, puffing out his chest.

"Me, either," Joey said, and swallowed hard.

Chapter

3

he sky was as black as midnight. The storm's fury was increasing every second. Thunder rolled through the sky. Wind rattled the windowpanes.

"I know what we can do!" Molly shouted excitedly. "Use the phone in the office! We can call our parents to come and get us!"

"Are you crazy?" cried Nate. "We don't want to call our parents, do we, Joey?"

"Of course not," said Joey, trying to sound braver than he felt.

"Well, *I* do! And you can't stop me!" Molly called over her shoulder as she ran from the room into the dark hallway.

The boys raced after her. There was no time

to find a light switch, and they stumbled through the corridors with only an occasional flash of lightning to show them the way.

"Oh, no! The phone's dead!" cried Molly, her voice shaking.

"So, what'd you expect?" Nate asked irritably. "And the electricity's probably out, too." He slapped the switch on the wall, and nothing happened. "See? What'd I tell you? You're stuck here, Molly Murphy, whether you like it or not. That's what you get for butting into our business."

Even in the semidarkness Joey could see that Molly was about to cry. Her chin was quivering, and she was scrubbing one eye with a fist.

He wouldn't admit it to Nate for a zillion dollars, but he sort of knew how she felt. His stomach flip-flopped and he jumped a foot every time thunder crashed or lightning streaked by the window. It surprised him to feel that way. He had thought riding out the storm in the school would be cool. Now he wasn't so sure.

"Hey, Powers. Let's break out the food! I'm starved," said Nate. He whirled around and started back down the hall toward the sixth-grade classroom.

As if on cue, Joey's stomach rumbled. There hadn't been time for a snack at home, which meant he hadn't eaten since before noon. He looked at the glowing numbers on his watch. 5:01.

Wow! he thought. It's almost supper time. No wonder I'm hungry.

He started after Nate and stopped, looking at his watch again. 5:02. The forecaster had said the storm would probably hit Ochopee at 5:52. That was less than an hour away! Suddenly he didn't feel hungry anymore.

When Joey got to the classroom, Nate had turned on his flashlight and had set it on Mr. Vernon's desk with the beam pointing toward the ceiling. He was pawing through his backpack and pulling out handfuls of cookies. Molly had her back to them, staring out the window at the raging storm.

Joey shuddered at the long, eerie shadow he cast in the flashlight's glow. It stretched out from his feet all the way across the room and halfway up the wall, looking like a dusky ghost. He shuddered again as he listened to the wild moan of the wind in the rafters. He hadn't expected the storm to be this bad, and the hurricane hadn't even hit Ochopee yet.

He cleared his throat a couple of times to start up his voice and then said, "Let's turn on the radio and see what they're saying about the storm now."

Nate's mouth was full of cookies, so he just nodded and flicked the switch on the boom box.

"*Leslie is moving closer to shore with sustained winds of 125 miles per hour and gusts of up to 140 miles per hour,*" the announcer was saying. Joey had to listen closely to make out the words because static popped and cracked loudly over the airwaves. "*The leading edge now is predicted to reach Ochopee at 5:35 P.M. instead of 5:52 P.M.*"

"5:35? Hey, that's early! And what does all that stuff about 125 miles an hour and 140 miles an hour mean?" asked Nate, his eyes huge with fright.

"It means we're *doomed*," Joey muttered.

Molly whirled around and crossed her arms over her chest, looking at the boys with disgust. "No, it doesn't, dummy. If you'd listened in class you'd have heard Mr. Vernon say that this school and most of the buildings in town can take winds of 150 miles per hour without collapsing. It's all very scientific. The worst that can happen is the windows will crash in and the roof will blow off."

"Oh, great! That's all, huh?" Nate asked, looking around fearfully.

18

"We'd better start getting ready," Molly instructed. "Let's put all of our supplies together under the teacher's desk, and—"

Suddenly the radio blared again. "*This is a special news bulletin just handed to me,*" said the announcer through the crackle of static. "*Ochopee police report that three local children are missing. Molly Murphy, Joey Powers, and Nathan Dolinsky, all sixth graders, have not been seen since mid-afternoon. A search was mounted for the children but had to be called off when authorities ordered all remaining citizens to evacuate and the town sealed off immediately because of the impending storm. I repeat: Three sixth-grade children from Ochopee are missing in the hurricane!*"

The children stared at each other in stunned silence for a minute. Joey tried to push away the pictures that were crowding into his mind. Boarded-up houses. Deserted streets. Not another solitary soul anywhere in town.

Then Nate cried frantically, "How could they do that? How could they just go off and leave us here? All alone!"

"Well, they did!" cried Joey. "You heard the man on the radio say so. I don't know what

19

we're doing here, anyway. I want to get out of here! I want to be with my family!"

"Don't blame me, Powers!" shouted Nate. "This was *your* idea! You thought it up, and now we're stuck in a stinking hurricane *all alone.*"

"Hey, guys," Molly said in a trembling voice. She had turned around and was looking out the window again. "Come here."

"What for?" grumbled Joey. She was probably going to show them something scientific. Big deal!

"I said come here," she demanded. "We're *not* alone! There's something dark coming out of the swamp!" Gasping, she pointed a shaky finger toward the darkness outside. "I can't tell what it is, but it's *heading toward us!*"

Chapter

4

Joey's heart stopped. "What . . . what do you mean . . . there's something out there that's . . . that's coming out of the swamp? What is it?"

"Just come here and look," Molly pleaded in a high, thin voice. "There's a big black shape *right there*. Beside the swings. See? It's stopped moving now and it's crouched down, like it's waiting for something."

Nate raced to the window. "Cool!" he shouted. "Maybe we've got ourselves a swamp monster." He laughed a sinister laugh and rubbed his hands together as if they were playing a spooky game. But when he peered through the rain, he gasped and looked thunderstruck. "Gross! Look at its mouth! It's all bloody!"

Joey took a couple of steps forward and stopped. He really didn't want to see what they were looking at. "Maybe it's the cops or somebody looking for us?" he said hopefully.

Molly shook her head and looked at him with terror in her eyes. "No, it isn't," she insisted. "I don't think it's *human*!"

Nate giggled nervously. "Hey, maybe it's old man Johnson's dog. Whatta ya bet?"

"I don't want to bet! I want it to go away!" yelled Molly.

Joey scrambled to the window. Through the pouring rain he could barely make out a heavy shape beside the swings. He blinked hard, trying to see it more clearly. Then lightning streaked across the sky. In the flash he caught a quick glimpse of something. But what? Was it a gigantic toad? Or was it a human, squatting close to the ground? Maybe it was some creep, trying to scare them.

Suddenly a bolt of lightning stabbed the transformer on top of the electric pole outside the window, exploding it in a neon flash of blue. Joey drew a deep breath and watched showers of sparks, like blue fireworks, mushroom into the air and rain back to the ground.

Molly grabbed Joey's arm. "It's gone!" she

said incredulously. "It was there a second ago, but now it's gone!"

"Maybe it . . . well, maybe we just thought we saw something," offered Joey. "This storm has really got us spooked." He liked that idea better than something that wasn't human creeping up on the school while they were in there alone.

"I did *too see* it!" she insisted, pointing out the window again and bouncing up and down on the balls of her feet. "Right there. Right beside the swings. Nate saw it. Ask him."

"Probably old man Johnson's dog, like I said," muttered Nate. He paced around the room, swinging his arms back and forth, as if he was loosening up his muscles.

Joey had seen him do that before. It usually happened when Nate was trying to convince himself not to be scared of something. Like the time the two of them had been jumped by a bunch of older boys from Everglade City who threatened to beat them up. Nate had loosened up while Joey had talked the boys out of it.

Joey checked his watch. 5:25. Only ten more minutes until the hurricane was due to hit. His scalp prickled with fear. He wished he could loosen up like Nate, but he knew it wouldn't help. Suddenly he had an idea.

23

"Hey, want to tell monster stories?"

Molly and Nate looked at him as if he'd lost his mind.

"Are you crazy?" said Molly. "You want to tell monster stories with that thing out there? We don't even know what it is—or *what it wants!*"

"Don't you remember what we do at camp?" Joey insisted. "We always tell stupid monster stories to keep from getting scared of the real stuff, you know, the dark and the creepy sounds in the woods."

"Forget it, Powers," warned Nate.

"Okay, okay. It was just an idea," said Joey.

"Is it still out there?" Molly asked nervously. "I'm scared to look."

Joey didn't want to look either, but he had to know. He took a deep breath and went to the window. At first all he saw was the wind-tossed trees. And debris flying through the air. But slowly his eyes focused on something off to the side moving slowly toward the school in short, jerky motions. Little tremors of fear tiptoed up his spine.

His mind raced. Maybe it was old man Johnson's dog, after all. It was about the right size. Then why didn't it find some shelter instead of hanging around out in the storm? Or maybe his mind was playing tricks on him, and it was just a black plastic garbage bag, being blown around by the wind.

Except the wind was blowing everything to the left. This thing was moving toward the school.

Joey swallowed hard and made himself look at it again. It had stopped moving.

It couldn't be a black plastic garbage bag. And it didn't look like a dog, either. It was too short and squat to be a dog. He shivered as he watched the rain wash down the sides of its slimy body. So what was it?

"Um, Molly. Come here," he said, trying to keep his voice from giving away his fear. She was smart. Maybe she could figure out what it was.

Molly had started digging things out of her dilapidated grocery bag and lining them up on Mr. Vernon's desk. So far there was a box of crackers, a jar of peanut butter, and a box of breakfast bars.

She gave Joey a frightened look. "What for? Not if it's about that thing out there. I don't want to look anymore."

"I want to ask you something. Come on," he urged.

25

Suddenly the thing turned a shadowy face toward the window. Joey gasped and shrank against the wall. Its mouth *was* bloody! Its eyes were gleaming, and it was looking straight at him!

At the same instant the hurricane hit with all its fury. The howl of the wind exploded with a roar that sounded like an approaching freight train.

Windows popped and shattered, showering the floor with glass.

Rocks and debris pelted the outside walls of the building.

Somebody screamed. In the roar of the storm, Joey couldn't tell if it was Molly or Nate.

Wind was coming in through the broken windows, swirling papers into the air.

"Come on!" he shouted. "Get all the stuff, and let's get out of this room! We've got to get as far away from these windows as we can!"

Everybody went into action. Molly stuffed the small jar of peanut butter into her jeans pocket and gathered the rest of her groceries in her arms. Nate took his flashlight from the desk and grabbed his boom box and backpack. Joey picked up his backpack from the floor. Herding together like frightened mice, the three groped their way through the darkness to the other side of the building.

But the rooms were in chaos on that side, too. Wind gusted in through the windows. Broken glass crunched underfoot.

"What if it comes around to this side and finds us?" wailed Molly.

"I know," said Joey. "The central hall by the principal's office. There aren't any windows there."

"But it's pitch-black," argued Molly.

"I've got my flashlight," said Nate. "Come on!"

A moment later they were in the central hall, sitting in the small circle of light from the flashlight, nibbling peanut butter-and-jelly sandwiches. Outside the storm raged on.

Nate let out a big sigh. "This is a lot better," he said. "I'm not even scared anymore."

Joey thought of the terrible hurricane bearing down on them.

He thought about how worried his parents must be right now.

And he thought of the black slimy thing crouching outside in the darkness. The thing with the bloody mouth.

"Me, either," he lied.

Chapter

5

"**T**urn on the radio," ordered Molly. "Let's see what they're saying about the storm now."

Nate flicked the switch on the boom box and turned up the volume so that they could hear it over the storm.

"*Hurricane Leslie has now made landfall and is devastating the tiny town of Ochopee on the edge of the Florida Everglades, where three sixth graders are missing and presumed dead—*"

"Dead!" all three cried in unison. They looked at one another in alarm.

Nate picked up his radio. "Hey, stupid, we're not dead!" he yelled back at it. "We're right here in the school! Come and get us!"

The announcer went right on talking. *"Because of the intensity of the storm, trees and dangerous live power lines are down all over the region. Authorities say it may be days before crews can clear away all the downed power lines and make it safe for residents to return to their homes."*

"Days?" Joey asked fearfully. "How can it take days?"

"Yeah," said Nate. "I'm going home as soon as the storm's over."

"Go ahead and get electrocuted. See who cares," said Molly, giving him a bored look.

"I could get around a bunch of stupid power lines without getting electrocuted any day of the week," bragged Nate.

"Oh, yeah?" Molly said back, making a face at him.

Joey was only half listening to Molly and Nate argue. He was thinking about spending days trapped in the school. And about the black shape out by the swings. Was it still there?

He tried to convince himself that it had just been their imagination. Nothing to worry about—just something blown there by the storm. In fact, it was probably gone now. Blown somewhere else. Maybe even out of town.

But he knew better. It was alive. And it knew that he and Nate and Molly were in the school.

He tossed down his half-eaten sandwich and got to his feet. Molly and Nate were too busy arguing to notice him slip down the dark hall toward the sixth-grade room.

It would only take him a minute to look out the window and see for himself if the thing was still there or if it had crawled back into the swamp. If he saw that it was gone, he could relax and just worry about surviving the storm and getting back to his parents.

When he opened the classroom door and stepped inside, it was like walking into a cyclone. Horizontal sheets of rain blew in through the broken windows, and water was ankle-deep on the floor. Debris was swirling around the room as if it were in a blender. Books had been knocked off shelves by the force of the wind.

Joey ignored it all. With his hands in front of his face for protection, he leaned against the wind and headed toward the nearest window. He had to see for himself. He *had* to know if the thing was still out there.

With his heart in his throat, he peered out into the darkness. At first he couldn't see anything but rain and blowing trees. Then he began to make out objects flying through the air. A chair. A car door. Things he couldn't identify. Big things, small things—all tumbling through the sky and rolling across the ground as if tossed by a giant invisible hand.

Joey tried to find the swing set in all the chaos. He strained to focus, looking toward the spot where it had always stood. Then he frowned.

It was gone! Vanished.

He looked even harder and finally spotted a tangled mass of metal a few yards from the building. It was the swing set, bent and twisted by the force of the hurricane and lying on its side.

"Wow!" he cried.

He started to turn away when he noticed something near the crumpled metal.

He looked again and sucked in his breath.

It was a black shape against a blacker night, squatting in the midst of the storm's fury like some primitive animal.

Pulsing. Waiting.

And it had grown.

31

Chapter

Joey slowly backed away from the window. Debris crashed against the walls. Wind roared through the rafters, sounding as if it would rip the roof off the school any second.

The instant he yanked open the door the wind picked up even more. It followed him into the hall and slammed doors up and down the corridor.

"Nate! Molly!" he cried at the top of his lungs.

His voice was lost in the wind, which was now growing louder. It sounded as if it were stomping down the hall after him. A thousand stampeding buffalo. Doors flew open. Slammed closed. Flew open. Slammed closed.

Joey put his hands over his ears and careened toward the central hall as fast as he could.

Just as he rounded the final corner and found Nate and Molly huddled together in the glow of the flashlight, everything stopped.

The wind stopped blowing. Doors stopped slamming. The vicious pelting on the roof and sides of the building stopped. It was totally quiet. The sudden stillness was bone chilling.

The three children stood frozen in silence, staring at each other.

Suddenly Nate exploded in excitement. "It's over!" he shouted, jabbing a fist sky high. "Yes! We made it!"

"It's not over, you dummy," snapped Molly. "It's the eye of the storm."

"What are you talking about?" Joey asked in amazement.

Molly snorted in disgust. "If you'd paid attention in class, you'd know. A hurricane is a giant, whirling storm, like a huge tornado, and in the middle it's deadly quiet. There's no wind. Nothing. That's called the eye of the storm. But the whole storm is moving, so the eye of the storm will also pass over us. In a little while the wind will start blowing all over again, just like it did before."

"You mean this is like an intermission?" asked Joey.

Molly nodded.

"Then how much time do we have before it starts blowing again?" asked Joey.

"Just a few minutes," replied Molly. "The storm moves pretty fast."

"I'm outta here!" yelled Nate. "I'm going *home!*"

He scrambled to pick up his backpack, stuck his boom box under his arm, and reached for his flashlight.

Molly grabbed it first and held it out of his reach. "You're crazy! You can't go out there," she cried. "Have you forgotten about the power lines? And you can't take the flashlight and leave Joey and me in the dark!"

Nate lunged for the flashlight, but Molly quickly jumped back.

"I told you, I'm not scared of any stupid power lines," said Nate, his face flushed with anger. "I'm going home, and you can't stop me. And give me that flashlight! If you don't want to come, you can sit in the dark, for all I care."

"Listen up, Nate," said Joey. He could feel his pulse pounding in his temples. "You can't go out there, and it's not just because of the power lines."

Nate threw him a questioning look.

34

"*It* is still out there," Joey went on. "I saw it again. Just now, while you two were arguing."

Both Molly and Nate were staring at him.

"The hurricane's wrecked everything. Stuff's blown all over the place. Even the swing set's all bent and mangled. But *it's* still there. It's just crouching out there in the middle of the storm like it's waiting." Joey lowered his voice and looked each of them straight in the eye. He didn't know exactly how to say what he was thinking, but he had to try. "I think Molly was right when she said it's something that crawled out of the swamp. It's shaped sort of like a toad. But it's not like anything I've ever seen before. Maybe the storm caused it. Maybe it's some kind of mutant. I don't know. But I swear, guys, it's bigger than it was before."

"Ha! You're pretty funny, Powers," said Nate. He raised his hands into the air and staggered around the hall like a crazed monster. "Look at me, everybody! I'm *the thing from the swamp!*"

He slapped his thigh and threw back his head, laughing hysterically.

"Cut it out, Nate," muttered Joey. "I'm serious."

"Oh, yeah? You know what I think? I think you're just trying to scare me so that I won't go off and leave you guys alone. I saw it before. And I still think it's old man Johnson's dog."

35

"If you don't believe me, I'll show you," challenged Joey. "Come on. You can look out our classroom windows and see it for yourself."

Nate gave him a long, hard look and then shook his head. "You're stalling. You just want me to hang around until the wind starts blowing again and I can't leave."

"No, he isn't," insisted Molly. "Don't forget I was the one who saw it first. I know how creepy it is. If Joey says it's gotten bigger, I believe him."

She glanced down the hall toward the sixth-grade room and shuddered. "How much bigger is it, Joey?"

"Come on. I'll show you," he said.

Joey led the way down the hall. In the quiet of the eye of the storm his footsteps sounded like thunder. Molly tiptoed along behind him. After a couple of minutes, Nate came, too.

Moonlight was streaming in the windows when they reached the room. Stars twinkled as if there had never been a storm. The three children moved cautiously toward the windows.

Joey gasped as he took in the devastation. Huge trees had blown over on their sides. The chain-link fence around the baseball diamond was twisted like a ribbon. The roof from the house across the street lay in the center of the school grounds. The grass was covered with rubbish.

His eyes swept over all the debris and stopped at the swing set. It was even more twisted and mangled than before. But something else was wrong.

"Where is it?" asked Molly.

"Yeah? I thought you said there was a monster out there," scoffed Nate. "See? I knew you were bluffing. Like I said before, I'm outta here!"

"Wait! You can't go!" cried Joey. "I wasn't bluffing. And I wasn't making it up, either. It's out there. I know it is. The only trouble is, now we don't know where."

Molly's eyes got big. "It could be anywhere!"

CRASH!

The sound had come from the room next door.

"What was that?" Molly whimpered.

Joey stared mutely at the wall separating the two rooms. He knew that the windows must have been blown out in there, too.

But the wind wasn't blowing now. Everything was deadly still.

That could only mean one thing.

"It's in the building!" he whispered.

Chapter

The kids clung together and listened in terror. Whatever it was, it was stomping around the room, smashing broken glass under its feet. It sounded like desks were being overturned. Things were being thrown against the walls.

Joey knew one thing for certain. The monster was mad!

"We've got to get out of here while we still can," he whispered.

Nate and Molly nodded and stared at the door without moving. Joey knew what they were thinking. If they tried to leave, the monster might hear and come after them.

There was always the window. But shards of

glass stuck up from the sills like gleaming knives. And even if they made it out that way, it would be easy for the monster to look out the windows of the room he was in and see them trying to escape.

No. There was only one choice. They had to leave by the door. And fast.

Joey nodded toward it. "Come on," he whispered.

Neither Nate nor Molly moved.

"Hurry up! It's the only way out," he urged.

Stepping around the broken glass on the floor, Joey made his way to the door, opened it a crack, and looked out into the silent hall. The door to the room where the monster raged was closed.

So far so good, he thought.

Holding his breath, he motioned for his friends to follow him. They slipped through the halls like frightened shadows, collapsing against the door once they were outside.

"What if he follows us?" asked Nate.

"He'll get electrocuted," said Molly. "Look at all those power lines on the ground."

"Yikes!" said Joey. "They look like a bunch of snakes!"

"Maybe some of them are," said Nate. "Remember how they come into town after a big

39

rain? Snakes and alligators, too. We'd better watch out for them."

Joey nodded. He didn't want to start out for home across deserted streets that could be full of snakes and alligators as well as electric lines. But he knew they couldn't go back into the school, either. And they had to hurry before the wind started up again.

The three children began cautiously picking their way toward home, stopping every so often to glance back anxiously at the school. In the moonlight the deserted landscape was an eerie shade of silver. Tall trees bent toward the ground and cast black, threatening shadows. Debris lay everywhere. But there was no sign of anything following them.

They reached Nate's house first. The boarded-up windows and doors made it look lonely and forsaken.

"Let's see if we can pull this piece of plywood off the door," said Nate.

He and Joey grabbed the board on one side, and Molly grabbed the other side. Together they tugged and pulled, but the board held fast.

"What about trying a window?" suggested Joey. "Maybe your dad didn't nail them down as tight."

"We'd better hurry," warned Molly. "I think the wind is starting to pick up again."

They went all the way around the house, but they couldn't break in. It was boarded up too securely.

Next they raced to Molly's house, but they couldn't get in there either.

Just as they scooted next door to Joey's house, the wind really began to blow. Big raindrops splashed their faces as they dashed across the lawn.

"Let's split up," said Nate. "I'll take the front of the house. You each take a side."

"Here! I've found one!" shouted Joey. He was pulling at a loose board covering the kitchen window. The nail was bent and had barely penetrated the sill.

Lightning crashed and thunder rolled, but the three children kept working at the loose corner. They were soaked to the skin as they jerked and yanked, but they could only pull the plywood a few inches away from the sill.

"Maybe you can get in, Joey," said Molly. "You're pretty skinny. And if you can get in, maybe you can push the wood out far enough for Nate and me to get in, too."

Joey nodded and squeezed under the plywood. It was tight, but he finally managed to open the window, slither over the sill like a snake, and drop onto the kitchen table. A few moments later all three were safely inside.

"Let's put some furniture over this window so that nothing else can get in here with us," Joey said over the pounding of his heart. He didn't say the word *monster*, but he knew both Nate and Molly knew that was what he meant.

They pushed aside the table and heaved and slid the tall sideboard full of dishes in front of the boarded-up window, fitting it closely against the wall.

"There," Joey said with satisfaction when the sideboard was firmly in place. "That should keep *everything* out."

When the full fury of the storm hit again, it was worse than before. The children huddled in a closet near the front door.

"It feels like the whole house is moving," cried Joey.

"Yeah, and my ears are popping," said Nate.

"The walls are sucking inward!" shouted Molly. "The roof's going to explode right off the house!"

"What if it does? What if the monster really did follow us . . . and he climbs over the walls and gets in?" Nate asked fearfully.

"We don't know if he followed us," Joey

insisted. "We kept looking behind us on our way here, but we didn't see anything. Remember?"

Molly's eyes were huge. "But what if he did, and we just didn't see him?"

"Yeah," said Nate. His lips were trembling as he spoke. "And what if he traps us in here? He could drag us back into the swamp and—"

"Shut up, Nate!" cried Joey. "Right now we're safe! Okay?"

They clung together for what seemed like hours, straining to listen in the deafening roar of the storm for the sound of the monster trying to break in.

Slowly the storm began to die down. Thunder rolled farther and farther away like a giant bowling ball heading down an alley. The wind changed from the sound of a stampede overhead to a whistling in the rafters. The pounding rain softened to a drizzle.

Finally all was quiet except for the frantic beating of their hearts. Joey opened the closet door and cautiously peered.

The house was still standing. The roof was still above them. The storm was over. Morning had come, and the monster was nowhere to be seen!

It was a while before they had the nerve to push aside the sideboard and look out the window into the orange glow of the rising sun.

43

"Do you see him? Is he out there?" Molly asked anxiously from behind Joey.

"I'm not going out there unless the coast is clear," said Nate.

Joey looked around before he spoke, slowly taking in the entire landscape.

"Gross! it looks like a garbage truck exploded all over everything!" he cried, pushing the plywood open and climbing outside. There was more devastation than he could ever have imagined. Rubbish littered the landscape for as far as the eye could see. "But I don't see the monster," he added solemnly.

Molly and Nate ventured out behind him.

"Look, there aren't any trees standing anymore," Molly said in awe. "And telephone poles and power poles are scattered around like toothpicks."

"And look at all the clothes and car parts," said Nate, reeling in disbelief. "And screen doors and roof shingles and—" He stopped suddenly and narrowed his eyes, looking in the direction of the school. "I just hope our parents get back soon."

Joey knew what Nate was thinking. Had the monster gone back into the swamp? Or was it still in the school?

"Me, too," he whispered. "The sooner the better."

Chapter

The kids had left their survival supplies in the school when they had escaped from the monster. Now they were starving.

"How about if we raid the kitchen?" Nate asked hopefully as he patted his round stomach. "I'll die if I don't get something to eat pretty soon."

"Your mom sure cleaned out the fridge," said Molly a minute later. "Nothing in here except dill pickles, ketchup, and mustard."

"Let's check the pantry," said Joey.

Since there was no electricity to heat anything, they opened jars of ravioli and spaghetti and ate them cold, right out of the jar. Joey found half a loaf of bread and made a stack of ketchp-and-mustard sandwiches, and Molly and Nate stuffed

45

handfuls of sugarcoated cornflakes into their mouths for dessert.

They were just finishing eating when Nate cocked his head.

"What's that?" he said. "I think I hear something."

Molly's eyes widened with alarm. "I do, too. It's low and rumbling like—"

"Yeah, like a *bulldozer* or something," Joey said excitedly. "I bet there are trees down across the road!"

"And somebody's trying to get through! Yippee!" Nate cried, leaping into the air. "We're going to be rescued!"

Molly jumped up, too. "Come on. Let's go meet him. He can find our parents and tell them we're not dead!"

Molly and Nate headed for the window where the plywood had been pulled loose, but Joey hung back, frowning.

"What's the matter?" Nate grumbled. "Don't you want to get out of here?"

Joey shrugged. "Maybe we should wait for them to find us," he said. "I mean, the power lines are still down out there and . . . you know . . . the thing from the swamp. It might still be out there, too."

"But it could still find us first," said Nate. "I think we should go get help."

"Me, too," said Molly.

"Okay," Joey said, looking uncertain. "But we've got to stick together."

The three children cautiously climbed out through the window. Outside, they slowly crept across the front lawn, stopping amid the debris to listen again.

"That definitely sounds like a bulldozer," Nate said excitedly. "And it's coming from the main road into town. Come on. What are we waiting for?"

Molly grabbed his arm. "You're forgetting something important, Nate," she said. The scared look had returned to her face. "To get to the bulldozer we'll have to go past the school."

Joey held up his hand for quiet. The bulldozer sounded louder now. That meant it was coming toward them. He was willing to take a chance on being spotted by the monster if it meant they could get help. There was no way an old swamp monster would be a match for a bulldozer!

"We'll just have to be careful," he said.

Joey swiveled his head in every direction and kept his ears tuned like antennae as they climbed over and through the junk piled helter-skelter all

47

over the streets. Gradually they inched their way toward the sound of the bulldozer.

Suddenly Nate stopped. "What's that?" he whispered, panting. "I saw something move over there!"

Joey's heart jumped into his throat, and cold sweat broke out on his forehead. He looked toward the tangle of boards and shingles where Nate was pointing and let out a big sigh of relief.

"It's just somebody's old jacket, blowing in the breeze," he said with a nervous laugh.

"Don't forget the power lines," cautioned Molly. She made a wide arc around an ominous-looking long black cable curled up in the grass like a sleeping snake.

They moved slowly through the deserted streets.

"It sure feels weird," mumbled Nate. "Like everybody's dead."

"Yeah, it reminds me of that movie where an atomic bomb blew up the world," said Joey.

"Don't say that!" shouted Molly, her voice echoing off the boarded-up buildings.

They rounded the next corner and stopped in their tracks. Standing silently in front of them was the school building. The shingles had been blown from the roof and were scattered all over the ground. The front door hung at a strange angle, like a gaping mouth. But worst of all were the windows, glass gone, looking like vacant, sightless eyes. The school they had been so used to almost looked like a monster itself.

Joey swallowed hard. "I don't see any signs of the thing. Do you?" he whispered.

Molly and Nate shook their heads in unison.

"Not yet, anyway," Nate whispered back.

"It could be in there," Molly said in a high, thin voice. "It could be watching us right now."

Joey remembered the shadowy face with the bloody mouth and shuddered. "Let's not waste any more time. Let's get going!"

Crouching low, the trio started to sneak past the school. Joey led the way toward the sound of the bulldozer. He kept one eye on the building as he hurried by the swings, the slide, and the other playground equipment, all twisted into grotesque shapes.

Suddenly Molly let out a gasp and clamped a hand over her mouth. Her other hand trembled as she pointed behind the school.

Joey's eyes were wide with fear. Something brown and slimy was hanging over the side of the Dumpster; the end where its head should be was buried in the garbage.

He wanted to run. But instead he blinked and looked closer. It was brown and slimy like something out of the swamp, all right.

But its short, fat legs had feet like a human!

Chapter

Joey had never moved so fast in his life. He bounded over mountains of trash, wrecked automobiles, and twisted metal. Nate and Molly were right behind him. He didn't care how much noise they made. The monster hadn't crawled back into the swamp. It was still at the school! And it could raise its head out of that Dumpster and spot them any second!

His lungs were bursting as his legs pounded the sidewalk. A pain in his side slowed him down for a moment, but chugs of smoke in the distance gave him a new burst of energy. The bulldozer was not far away.

"Help!" he cried as he crashed through the underbrush and into the path of a big yellow machine. "Help!"

Nate and Molly waved their arms, trying to flag down the driver. Another bulldozer was not far behind.

Suddenly the first driver spotted them. He cut the engine and leaned out of the cab. He was a big man with a cigar stuck in the side of his mouth. "Hey, you kids! What are you doing here? Are you the ones who are missing?"

Joey nodded. "We're okay. We rode out the storm in the school. But there's this monster—" he yelled breathlessly, "something out of the swamp. He tried to get us! We got away! But he's still in the school!"

Nate ran up beside him. "That's right! We just saw him eating out of the Dumpster! He's fat and brown and slimy with blood all over his face!"

"Okay, okay," said the driver of the second bulldozer. He had climbed down and was leaning against the blade of his machine. "Calm down. You're so scared, you're imagining things. Don't worry. You're gonna be okay."

"Right, Charlie," said the other driver. "You settle 'em down, and I'll radio the Highway Patrol and let 'em know the kids are safe."

"But you don't understand!" cried Molly. "We're *not* imagining things! We saw it!"

52

The driver named Charlie wiped his face with a red bandanna and looked at the children earnestly. "Now, slow down, and let's start at the beginning. We'll get to your monster in a minute. You said you rode out the storm in the school? Why did you do a thing like that? Why didn't you evacuate with your families?"

Joey tried to answer Charlie, but his mind was a whirlwind. The two men weren't listening to them.

"It was because . . . I mean, me and Nate . . . we have this game we play to see who's the bravest . . . but this thing was outside the window and it was black—" he gulped in a breath and went on, "and its mouth was bloody . . . and Molly saw it first . . . and we went into the hall to get away from it when the windows blew out—"

"Whoa!" said Charlie, holding up his hands in protest. "Didn't I say to slow down?" he asked, looking at each one of them.

All three kids nodded solemnly.

Charlie took a deep breath. "Now, for openers, there's no such thing as a monster. Okay? Got that?"

"But—" said Molly.

Charlie shook his head and held up his hands again. "Trust me. You're gonna be fine. Burt's calling the Highway Patrol right now to let your parents know you're safe. And just as soon as we get this road open so that the power crews can get in to fix the lines, things'll start getting back to normal."

Joey exchanged nervous looks with Nate and Molly but didn't say anything. He knew there was no use.

"And I want you to promise me that there won't be any more monster talk," Charlie went on. "Promise?"

Joey glanced frantically back toward town. The monster was there, as sure as he was alive. But there was no use arguing with Charlie. He wouldn't believe them no matter what they said. The only people who might believe them were their parents.

"Okay," he said with a sigh. "We'll promise. Won't we, guys?" he said, giving both Nate and Molly warning looks.

They acted surprised, but they both murmured okay.

Just then Burt yelled, "Hey, kids, I got hold of the cops. They're relaying the message to your folks, and they're sending a squad car out here to get you."

When the mustard-and-black car with FLORIDA

HIGHWAY PATROL written on the side got there a little while later, an officer calling himself Sergeant Merrill greeted them warmly.

"Your parents got the news that you're safe a few minutes ago," he said. "I don't have to tell you, they've been worried sick. Now what's this I hear about a monster?"

Joey took a deep breath and told Sergeant Merrill as calmly as he could about the creature outside the window during the storm, and about how it had gotten into the school and they had had to make their way home during the lull in the storm to escape it. Finally he explained about the brown slimy thing with human legs and feet that they had just seen eating out of the Dumpster.

"You've got to believe us," he pleaded. "We really aren't making it up."

Sergeant Merrill smiled kindly. "I can see that," he said. "And I have a theory about your monster."

Joey gave him a startled look. "You do?"

The officer nodded. "I think you weren't the only ones who didn't evacuate Ochopee last night before the storm. I also think this creature you saw was somebody else trying to ride out the storm, and I'll bet he was just as scared as you were. You said his face was bloody. He was probably hurt. Maybe hit by flying debris. And he was hungry enough this morning to eat out of a Dumpster. I'll radio for backup and send them into town to try to rescue your friend."

Joey stared at the officer incredulously. *Friend!* He wanted to shout that the monster *wasn't* his friend. And that the last thing in the world they should do was try to rescue it.

But the words wouldn't come out.

Chapter

The police couldn't find the monster. Neither could anyone else. And like Charlie and Burt and Sergeant Merrill, their parents had determined that the thing the kids had seen was not a monster.

"It was probably just some poor traveler who got caught in the storm," Joey's mother had insisted when she heard the story. "What a shame no one can find him. I certainly hope he's okay."

So by the time the town was cleaned up from the storm and school was set to reopen, Joey, Nate, and Molly's monster story was the talk of Ochopee, and they were being teased unmercifully by their classmates. The three had decided to stick together for mutual protection, even though the boys had never liked Molly very much, and she felt the same about them.

"Hey, here come the Three Stooges!" yelled Todd Dooley, a freckle-faced kid with a big nose, on the first day back at school. Boys and girls were just beginning to gather on the school grounds.

"Yeah, the Three Stooges meet Frankenstein, just like in the movies!" shouted Mike Niles, Todd's best friend. Mike staggered around stiff-legged, with his arms held out like a monster.

"Look at me! I'm the monster from the swamp!"

Every kid within hearing range broke up laughing.

"You morons should have been there," Molly yelled back at the boys. "You act brave now, but you'd have been bawling your eyes out for your mommies."

"Is that what you did?" cried a voice from the crowd.

"Come on, let's just ignore them," urged Joey, moving away from the groups of kids who were laughing and pointing at them. "They're never going to believe us anyway."

"Oh, yeah? I'd like to punch their lights out," growled Nate.

"You're probably right about ignoring them, Joey," said Molly. "I just wish everybody would forget about it and do it soon."

"I still worry about what happened to the monster," Joey said. He glanced over to where the marshy swamp met the edge of town.

It had been almost a week since people had come back to their homes, and search parties had combed the town. But not one person had seen anything that looked like their monster. It made his skin prickle to think about it. "Do you guys think it really did crawl back into the swamp?"

"If it did, it could still be out there," said Nate. "And it could come back into town whenever it wants to."

"But what *was* it?" Molly asked. She put her hands on her hips and sighed impatiently. "My dad hunts wild pigs in the swamp all the time, and he said he never saw anything like what I described. Of course he thinks we were seeing things, like everybody else," she added angrily.

"Well, if you want my opinion," Joey said, "I think that monster is some kind of mutation. And *I* think it had something to do with the storm. Mr. Vernon was telling us about all the stuff that blows in from Africa and twirls around together in the sky over the ocean and sucks up water and sea life and stuff. What if it landed in the Everglades and got mixed up with the goo and slime there? Maybe something weird happened. You know, like a chemical reaction."

"Joey Powers, that's the stupidest thing you've ever said in your whole life!" shrieked Molly. "It's totally *un*scientific! You've been watching too many Saturday morning cartoon shows."

"Okay, then, what is it?" Joey challenged. "You're so smart. Explain the thing from the swamp!"

"Yeah," said Nate. "Go ahead."

"I . . . I can't," she admitted. "Not yet, anyway. But I know there's got to be a scientific explanation, and *I'm* going to find out what it is," she said scornfully. "So there!"

The bell rang before either boy could reply.

As Joey stepped inside the classroom, he looked around nervously. The last time he had been there it had been pitch-dark. The wind had been gusting in through the broken windows, and glass had crunched underfoot. But that wasn't all. The monster had been there, lurking outside in the storm.

Now everything was back in perfect order.

The sun was shining. The windows had been repaired, the glass swept away. And books were piled neatly on Mr. Vernon's desk, just as they had been before the storm.

But he still couldn't help feeling something was wrong.

The man sitting behind Mr. Vernon's desk wasn't Mr. Vernon.

Nate poked Joey in the ribs. "Who's that guy?" he whispered from behind his hand.

Molly swung around and looked at him in surprise. "Where's Mr. Vernon?" she asked.

"Beats me," said Joey.

He looked closely at the man sitting in Mr. Vernon's chair, gazing at a book that was open on the desk. He was short and plump, and he wore a brown leather suit. Joey had never seen anyone in a brown leather suit before. The man's hair was brown, too, and it was parted in the middle and slicked back from his face, where a row of warts zigzagged across his forehead. He had a wide mouth, slightly bulging eyes, and a soft, pulsing neck.

Definitely one weird dude, Joey thought.

"Good morning, boys and girls," the man said in a deep, hoarse voice when everyone was seated and the final bell had rung. He closed the

61

book and got slowly to his feet. "My name is Mr. Batrachian, and I'm your new sixth-grade teacher. Unfortunately Mr. Vernon was called away on personal business just after the storm, and I have been asked to take his place for the time being."

He smiled softly. His eyes blinked rapidly and darted around the class. Joey thought he saw them flicker and his mouth move ever so slightly when they stopped on him. He shuddered. But then the teacher's eyes moved on around the room.

"Yessssss, we're going to get along so well together," he said in his deep voice as he walked up and down the rows of desks, smiling approvingly. "I feel so fortunate to be your new teacher. I *love* working with boys and girls, and I hope I'll be able to open your eyes to the wonders of learning and give each and every one of you experiences you've never dreamed of having."

He paused, rubbing his hands together as if imagining what great times they were going to have. Then he started walking again.

All around the room, kids were looking the new teacher over and screwing their faces into puzzled expressions. They looked at one another and shrugged as if to say exactly what Joey had been thinking: The new teacher is weird.

Joey looked up, startled, when Mr. Batrachian walked past his desk and a faint, musty odor drifted into his nostrils.

"Yessssss, boys and girls, we're going to go into the Everglades on field trips to study the ecosystem and learn how the hurricane has changed the balance of nature," the teacher was saying. His eyes gleamed. "I'll bet your former teacher never took you on field trips to the Everglades, did he?" asked Mr. Batrachian, nodding his head knowingly.

Slowly smiles spread across the students' faces. They nodded to one another.

"Yeah! Wow!"

"Field trips!"

Mr. Batrachian held up his hands. "Quiet, pleasssssse."

Everyone got quiet immediately, but kids squirmed in their seats and grinned at each other.

Joey didn't squirm and he didn't grin. The other kids might have decided Mr. Batrachian was okay when he promised field trips, but something about the new teacher was making him nervous. He glanced at Nate and Molly. They looked as happy as the rest of the class.

63

"And the very first field trip . . ." The teacher's voice trailed off, and his eyes focused on a fly circling in the air in front of his face.

Joey watched him closely as his long thin tongue played along the edges of his lips.

Suddenly he jerked, as if he was coming out of a trance.

"The very first field trip will be tomorrow," said the new teacher. "Here are your permission slips. Take them home, get them signed by your parents, and bring them to school in the morning." He sent a handful of slips down each row.

At lunchtime the cafeteria was full of talk about Mr. Batrachian. So much talk that no one teased Joey, Nate, and Molly about their monster.

"At first I thought Mr. Batrachian was creepy," said Todd Dooley. He was sitting at the table next to Joey and his friends, talking to Mike Niles and a couple of other boys.

"Me, too," said Mike. "He looks like a big fat toad in that brown leather suit."

"Yeah, warts and all," said Todd, laughing loudly. "But I changed my mind about him when he said we're going on field trips.

"Man, I think Mr. B. is cool," said Nate,

64

chomping on his bologna sandwich. "I can't wait until tomorrow. I hope we'll see tons of alligators. Hey!" he said, chewing a big bite of sandwich. "Maybe we can talk him into letting us bring a baby alligator back to school to raise as the class mascot! We could have a contest to name it!"

Todd's and Mike's eyes got big. "Yeah!" they said in unison.

"Gross," said Molly, wrinkling her nose. "Besides, if you knew anything about alligators, you'd know that mother alligators guard their nests and attack anybody or anything that gets near their babies. You'd be dead meat if you tried to steal a baby alligator."

"You wish," said Nate, giving her a superior look. "I can outsmart an alligator any day of the week, and I can do it with my eyes closed, my legs cut off, and my arms tied behind my back. Try me."

"Where have I heard that before?" Joey said sarcastically. It was Nate's favorite line.

"Well, I really like our new teacher, too," Molly went on, ignoring Nate. "So he looks a little different. Who cares? Looks aren't everything. Besides, we're going to learn so many new scientific things from him! School's going to be more fun than ever!"

Joey didn't join in the conversation. He was feeling a little uneasy. For one thing, he wasn't really into the slimy, crawly things that lived in the swamp, so he hated the thought of going into the Everglades. He wasn't even sure he could put up a good front. All he needed was more teasing from his classmates.

But what bothered him most was Mr. Batrachian. There was something he didn't quite like about that man. Maybe it was his looks. Or maybe it was the musty smell that clung to his clothes and the way his tongue flicked around his lips. Whatever it was, it made him think of the hurricane and the thing from the swamp.

Chapter

The next morning Joey packed himself two peanut butter-and-jelly sandwiches and an apple for lunch on the field trip and headed for school. He almost wished that his parents had refused to sign his permission slip, but naturally they hadn't.

"I think it's great that you have a new teacher who's willing to take you out to see the wonders of the Everglades firsthand," his mother had said, signing the slip with a flourish. Frowning, she added, "I never was that keen on Mr. Vernon."

"I agree," Mr. Powers chimed in. "Why, if you ask me, the Everglades ought to be one of the seven wonders of the world."

Joey sighed as he trudged along toward school. If the Everglades ought to be one of the seven wonders of the world, the way his dad had said, then Mr. Batrachian ought to be in the *Guinness Book of Records* as the world's weirdest teacher. Why did he wear a brown leather suit? And why did his dry, warty skin look as if it had been stretched too tightly across his face? Was that why his mouth was so wide? And his eyes. They were really strange.

He heard footsteps behind him and looked back to see Molly rushing to catch up with him.

"What does she want?" he grumbled under his breath.

"Hi, Joey. Aren't you excited about our field trip today?" she began the instant she was beside him.

"No," he said nastily. He just wished she'd go away and leave him alone.

"Well, I am," she went on, as if he'd invited her to make a speech. "And you would be, too, if you knew more about the Everglades. For instance, do you know how it got its name?"

Joey rolled his eyes. "No, but I'll bet you're going to tell me."

"Of course I'm going to tell you. You need to know this stuff," she said, and pushed her glasses up on her nose. "The swamp makes up only a small part of the Everglades. Most of it is marshland, thousands of acres of flooded saw grass. The Indians discovered it first and called it *Pa-hay-okee*, or 'the grassy waters.' A *glade* is a grassy area, and since it seems to go on forever, people started calling it the Everglades. Now isn't that interesting?"

Joey ignored her. So what if there were thousands of acres of flooded saw grass in the Everglades? They were going into the swamp part with Mr. Batrachian, and it was making his skin crawl just to think about it.

Nate was waiting for them at the edge of the school grounds.

"Look at this," he said proudly, holding up a burlap bag. "I brought it to take on the field trip. I can carry a baby alligator home in it, if I find one."

"Get serious, Dolinsky," said Joey, shaking his head.

"Well, I could," argued Nate. "I read in the paper once about a man in Miami who kept a pet alligator in his house for twenty-four years. He named her Gwendolyn, and she weighed two hundred pounds. Honest."

"That's the stupidest thing I ever heard," Molly snapped.

69

Joey wasn't interested in any more conversation about pet alligators. He left Nate and Molly arguing and slipped around the side of the school and up to the windows of his room. He wanted to get another look at the new teacher on the sly.

He raised his eyes over one of the windowsills. He could see Mr. Batrachian sitting at the desk, reading a small, thin book. The teacher wasn't aware that he was being spied on, and he nodded and smiled contentedly as he read. Because of the way Mr. Batrachian was holding the book, Joey could only make out the last word of the title: *CHILDREN.*

Probably a child psychology book, Joey thought. Teachers were always reading stupid stuff like that.

Right after the bell rang, Mr. Batrachian collected the permission slips.

"Now, my lovely sssssstudents," he said in his deep voice. "We'll be going on our field trip into the Everglades in just a few minutes. But before we go, I'm going to hand out a sheet of paper to each one of you. On your sheet you'll find a picture and some information about one thing that's found in the Everglades. You are supposed to find the object on your sheet. Take the one on top and pass the rest back," he said.

70

Across the aisle, Nate got his first. "Gosh, I wanted an alligator, not a fiddler crab," he grumbled.

"I'm lucky. I got a bald eagle," Molly said proudly, passing the stack of sheets over her shoulder to Joey. "The bald eagle is the symbol of America."

Joey looked down at his sheet as he slid it off the top of the stack and passed the others back. "Strangler Fig" was written across the top of the page. The picture showed a cypress tree with a lacy-patterned root wrapped tightly around its trunk. Under the picture it said:

This strangler fig has a death grip on the host tree. Probably deposited as a seed in the upper branches by a bird, the downward spiraling roots will eventually spread their tentacles around every part of the tree and strangle it to death.

Joey shivered. Why couldn't he have gotten a fiddler crab or a bald eagle instead of something that sounded so sinister?

"Come on now, boys and girls, let'ssssss be on our way," said the teacher, motioning toward the door.

The class filed out slowly into the hot, humid sunshine. Joey hung back, letting all the other students go first. He dreaded this field trip more than ever now that he had gotten the strangler fig as his assignment. He wished there were some way he could get out of going.

But there wasn't.

He was the last one out of the building, and he glanced back at the teacher, who was shutting the school door behind him.

Suddenly Joey did a double take. He blinked, trying to be sure of what he had seen.

Just as Mr. Batrachian had shut the door, another fly had been circling in the air around his head. Joey was sure that a long, thin tongue had darted out of the teacher's mouth and pulled the fly inside.

Chapter

12

Joey hurried to catch up with Nate and Molly as the class left school and headed down the road toward the spot where the town of Ochopee ended and the swamp began.

"You're not going to believe this," he said in a low voice so no one near them could hear.

"Believe what?" asked Nate, without looking up. He was busy trying to stuff his burlap bag into the back pocket of his jeans.

Molly was giving him a questioning look, but suddenly Joey didn't quite know how to explain the crazy thoughts going through his mind. "It's about Mr. Batrachian," he began.

"If you're going to tell us he's weird again, forget it," Molly said. "He may be a little strange, but he's the best teacher we've ever had. He really acts like he cares about kids."

"Yeah," said Nate. "School's fun now. Not like when Mr. Vernon was here. All he did was try to cram a bunch of stupid facts down our throats. Bor-*ring*!"

"But haven't you noticed how he talks?" Joey went on. "He hisses sometimes, like some kind of reptile."

"He has a speech impediment," Molly said, frowning indignantly at Joey. "Don't you know it's impolite to point out things like that?"

"That's not all," Joey insisted. He couldn't understand why they were so blind. "Didn't you see the way his tongue flicks in and out of his mouth? And it isn't a regular tongue. It's funny looking. Long and skinny. Like a snake's tongue. Or a frog's. And just now I saw him flick it out and catch a fly. Then he ate it! I swear!"

"Gross," said Molly.

"You're seeing things, Powers," said Nate, giving him a look of disgust.

"Like I said, you watch too many Saturday morning cartoon shows," added Molly. "The next thing you'll be trying to tell us is that he's the thing from the swamp. I've made up my mind that we did dream that up, after all, like everybody says. There's no scientific basis for monsters. It's just plain nonsense—they *don't exist!*"

Her words startled Joey. "But what about the bloody mouth on the thing we saw? We *all* saw it, and you can't say we didn't," he argued.

"Forget it, Joey. We were pretty scared by the storm and the dark and all the noise," said Molly. "We could have just *thought* we saw a monster, bloody mouth and all."

"I'm with you, Molly," said Nate. "We were just spooked. The more I think about it, the more I know it's true. Wise up, Powers. Our new teacher is *not* something that crawled out of the swamp."

"I'm not trying to tell you Mr. Batrachian's a monster," Joey said quickly. "At least . . . I don't think so." Even with all his questions about the teacher, he wasn't quite ready to give in to an idea like that.

"Boyssssss and girlssssss, we're here," Mr. Batrachian called from the front of the line. "Let's all stay close together now as we venture into the beautiful swampland of the Everglades. Remember to look for the objects on your sheets. And watch where you step," he added with a soft laugh. "There are lots of little creatures who make their homes here, and they don't like to be disturbed."

He got a faraway look in his eyes and then said, "Remember, boysssssss and girlsssssss, it was in the swamp that life first crawled out of the sea to become the creatures who now inhabit the land."

The words sent an icy shaft of fear plunging to the pit of Joey's stomach. What did he mean by that? he wondered anxiously. Was he talking about himself?

With the teacher leading the way, they entered a strange new world. Nate and Molly rushed forward eagerly, but Joey hesitated. He peered around as he cautiously took a step onto the rain-soaked ground. He'd lived by the swamp all of his life and been in it lots of times. But now, after the hurricane, it looked strangely different.

The jungle of towering cypress and palm trees that had stood erect before the storm were tangled and twined together now; they turned the bright daylight to a dismal dusk. Spanish moss hung like forgotten laundry from the branches that remained on the cypress trees. A damp, murky smell—like decay—rose from the muck beneath Joey's feet.

He sniffed and wrinkled his nose in disgust. Then he sniffed again. It was the same odor he had smelled when Mr. Batrachian had walked past his desk the day before. He was sure. But there was no use telling Molly or Nate. They'd never believe him.

A great gray heron on long, sticklike legs waded among the cattails and eyed Joey warily before spreading its wings and flying away.

Joey jumped and whirled around. Had something behind him moved? He tensed and looked into the dense undergrowth, searching for eyes. An alligator's eyes. Or a snake's. Maybe a panther's or a black bear's. But nothing looked back at him. He shook off the eerie feeling and moved on.

"Don't forget your assssssignments, boys and girls." Mr. Batrachian's voice came from somewhere ahead of him.

Startled by how far away the teacher sounded, he splashed through the ankle-deep water and caught up with the rest of his class. This was not the sort of place where he wanted to get left behind.

They slogged through the swamp. Joey could feel mud oozing into his tennis shoes with every step.

Why didn't I wear my hiking boots? he wondered with a sigh.

Mr. Batrachian stopped and held up a hand. Then he pointed to a bushy tree that grew where the marshy ground gave way to a stream. "That tree is called a mangrove," said the teacher. "But the Indians called it a walking tree because it sticks its roots out like marching legs, plants them firmly in the mud, and moves ever so slowly toward the opposite bank. See?"

Joey and the others peered at the mangrove tree. Sure enough, short-stemmed legs were protruding from the branches. Some seemed to be tiptoeing into the water as if they really were walking. Other legs had plunged into the muddy depths, and new, smaller legs were already kicking off from the same branch.

"As time passes, those roots will take hold in the mud, and the walking tree will walk all the way across this stream, blocking the flow of water," said Mr. Batrachian as he and the class moved on.

Joey curved around the mangrove tree, eyeing it nervously as he went by. He didn't like the idea of trees that walked, even though all they did was plant their roots in the mud. It was creepy.

"Hey, Mr. Batrachian, I'm starving," called out Todd Dooley, wiping the sweat off his freckled face. "Can we eat lunch now?"

There was a chorus of "Yeah, Mr. Batrachian! We're starving!" from the class.

The teacher's face lit up in a smile. He blinked his eyes rapidly, and his long, skinny tongue flicked between his lips.

"Oh, yesssss, boys and girls," he said, rubbing his hands together in delicious anticipation. "I'm hungry, too, and I love food! Scrumptious, delicious, mouthwatering food! Let'ssssss eat!"

Joey looked in disgust at the fat little man in the brown leather suit. Maybe that's how he got so pudgy, he thought, and smiled grimly. He has a *monster* appetite.

The children followed the teacher to a small clearing and fanned out, looking for dry places to sit down and eat their lunches.

Joey started to join Nate and Molly and then changed his mind. He wasn't comfortable being around them anymore. Nate was supposed to be his best friend, and Molly was the obnoxious class brain. And the three of them had experienced the terror of the hurricane together and had seen the monster with their own eyes. Now suddenly they were saying that the monster had never happened. They were saying that they had all just been hallucinating the night of the storm! And now they were ganging up on him and accusing him of bad-mouthing the new teacher.

What's the matter with them, anyway? he thought. Are they blind? It wouldn't take a rocket scientist to see that Mr. Batrachian isn't your normal sixth-grade teacher. And yet everybody in the entire class had been taken in by him. Were they all blinded by the adventure of going on field trips into the Everglades? he wondered.

Well, I'm not taken in, and I'm not blinded by adventure, Joey thought stubbornly. And I don't believe that Mr. Batrachian is as great as everyone else thinks he is.

Joey found a dry rock at the edge of the clearing and sat down to eat his lunch alone. Most of the class sat around in groups. He didn't know where Mr. Batrachian had disappeared to, and he didn't much care.

Across the way, Nate and Molly were whispering together. And laughing. They were probably laughing about him, and it hurt—a lot!

He took a bite of his peanut butter-and-jelly sandwich and rolled it around in his mouth. It tasted like cement. It stuck like cement, too. He pulled the container of orange juice from his backpack, stuck in the straw, and sucked up a stream of juice into his mouth to loosen the cement. It helped, and he managed to swallow the gooey lump.

He took a second bite. It was no better than the first. And he could see Nate and Molly out of the corner of his eye. They were still whispering. And laughing.

Maybe I'll feed the rest of this crummy sandwich to the alligators, he thought.

Joey picked up both halves of his sandwich and stood up, following a path that led away from the clearing. He wouldn't go very far—just far enough to dump the sandwich.

Turning down the twisted path, he stopped in his tracks.

Mr. Batrachian was about ten feet away. His back was to Joey, and he was crouched like an animal, squatting so low that his knees came all the way up to his ears.

Joey looked closer and sucked in his breath. The teacher was gnawing on something that looked like a small raccoon.

And blood was smeared all over his face.

Just like the monster's face the night of the storm.

Chapter

For an instant Joey couldn't move. All he could do was stare at his teacher, his eyes wide with fright.

Mr. Batrachian was uttering low growls and gnawing hungrily at the lifeless carcass. He stopped only to spit out dark fur. Then he sank his teeth into his prey again, slurping loudly. Blood ran down his forearms and dripped off his elbows.

Ice-cold fear clutched Joey's heart. He took a deep breath and started backing away slowly— inch by inch—praying that Mr. Batrachian wouldn't notice him.

His arm brushed a mangrove tree, and its leaves rustled. Joey froze and held his breath. The teacher was so intent on devouring the animal that he tossed a bone onto the ground and went on eating without looking up.

Rounding a curve in the path, Joey whirled and broke into a run. Muck splashed onto his legs as his feet pounded through the shallow water. His lungs burned as he careened around one curve after another in the dense underbrush, knocking branches out of his way.

"Hey, everybody! Where are you?" he called frantically.

He swiveled his head from side to side, but the mangroves all looked alike. Where was everyone? He had only gone a few steps out of the clearing to throw away his sandwich.

His sandwich! Shooting a glance down at his clenched fist, he frowned in disgust. He had squashed it to a pulp, and brown and purple goo squeezed through his fingers like toothpaste from a tube.

On he ran, pumping his arms. He batted away long strands of Spanish moss that dangled from the trees and swept his face like cobwebs.

"Nate! Molly!" he yelled at the top of his lungs. "Somebody! Where *are* you? Where did you *go*?"

The only answer was the call of a seagull, screaming overhead.

"I'm lost!" Joey cried, sliding to a stop in the mud and gulping in great mouthfuls of air. He forced himself to try to calm down and look around slowly to see if he could spot something familiar.

The swamp was quiet, except for the low drone of mosquitoes. Even the saw grass stood erect without the slightest breeze to ruffle its daggerlike blades. Lily pads stretched out like a flagstone path across tea-colored water.

Joey struggled to get hold of himself. He took several deep breaths, and his pulse began to return to normal. He was lost, but at least Mr. Batrachian hadn't followed him. If he could only think straight, maybe he could figure out what to do next.

He stared into the murky water, watching a pair of water bugs zip back and forth like dizzy skaters. But as he stood there in a daze, he began to feel the presence of someone watching him.

It started as a creepy feeling. It made his skin crawl. Eyes. He could feel them on his face. He looked around frantically. Where were they coming from? Was someone lurking in the dense undergrowth? Maybe somebody from his class, playing a trick on him? Or was his teacher's face, with its bloody mouth, peering out between mangrove branches and following his every move?

He strained to catch a sound of someone sneaking up on him, though all he heard was the low drone of mosquitoes. But he still felt eyes on him—staring at him, boring into him. Joey's knees felt weak, and the blood in his veins seemed to turn into ice water.

He tried his best to look around casually by holding his head still and only moving his eyes. The eerie feeling was getting stronger, but he couldn't see anything. Sweat poured down from his forehead and stung his eyes.

"Who's there?" he called. The words came out in a breathy whisper and broke the silence. "Who's there?" he repeated a little louder.

No one answered.

Suddenly the water in front of him rippled. Nearby, lily pads rocked like tiny green cradles.

Joey gasped and backed away from the water.

Don't panic, he cautioned himself. It's probably just a big fish swimming by.

The swamp was full of fish. They were the main food supply of the tropical birds that nested in the trees. It was not unusual to see whole schools of fish churning the water.

Just a fish, he told himself.

But then his heart stopped.

Three points, shaped like a triangle, were emerging from below the surface of the water.

ALLIGATOR!

Joey wasn't sure if he screamed it out loud or inside his head. All he knew was that the piercing eyes he had sensed were rising out of the murky water behind the pointed snout of a giant reptile who was moving his way.

The body of the huge beast parted the water as it dragged itself up onto the land. It opened its giant mouth and let out a hiss like the sound of a thousand snakes.

Its mouth formed a sinister smile. Row after row of long, razor-sharp teeth glistened in the monstrous grin.

The gator must have been ten feet long. Its powerful tail lashed back and forth like a giant whip, mowing down bushes and flattening saw grass.

"Oh, no! Oh, no!" whimpered Joey, shaking his head frantically and backing away.

The alligator was out of the water now and racing toward him on short thick legs, its low-slung body carving a trench in the mud. The gleam in its eyes told Joey that he was going to be its next meal!

He looked around desperately for somewhere to run. He had always heard that alligators could move with lightning speed, even on land. There was nothing but mangrove thicket around him. He had lost the path he had come by.

He plunged into the bushes. Thorns and brambles tore at his face and clothes. He didn't care. He had to get away.

"Help!" he screamed. "Oh, please! Somebody help!"

Behind him, he could hear the crashing of the huge gator coming after him.

Suddenly the trees parted in front of him as if a pair of gigantic hands had opened curtains.

He fell, panting, into the clearing where his classmates sat finishing their lunches. Everybody stopped talking and looked at him in surprise.

"Hey, Powers. Where've you been?" asked Nate.

"I hope you have a good explanation," said Molly, looking down her nose at Joey, lying on the ground. "Mr. Batrachian is really steamed that you wandered off somewhere by yourself."

Joey struggled to catch his breath. "You'd better . . . look out . . . everybody! There's a giant bull alligator . . . heading this way, and . . . he's looking for *lunch*!"

Nate looked down at Joey and scoffed. "Hey, everybody! Did you hear that? Joey says an alligator's going to eat us! I'm sure Mr. Batrachian is going to buy a loony story like that!" He threw back his head and laughed.

"I'm *not lying!*" Joey insisted. "He's after me. And he's moving fast!"

"In your dreams, Powers," said Mike Niles, grinning at his best friend Todd Dooley as if he were some kind of expert on Joey's dreams.

"What'sssss going on here?"

Joey jerked around in horror to see Mr. Batrachian standing behind him. The teacher was smiling kindly at him. The blood was gone from his face and arms. No dark tufts of raccoon hair clung to his lips or his brown leather suit.

"I . . . I was running away . . . away from an alligator," Joey stammered. "Over there!" He pointed to the direction he had come from. "Can't you hear him?"

Mr. Batrachian cocked an ear. Everyone got still. They watched mutely as a few seconds later the teacher disappeared into the underbrush Joey had just trampled through.

"What's happening?" asked Molly.

"Yeah, where's he going?" said Nate, looking around in confusion.

88

Joey ignored both of them. He was listening hard for sounds of the beast. The swamp was silent as a tomb. All he could hear was his pulse pounding in his temples.

Where was the gator now? It would surely be here any second!

But instead of the alligator, Mr. Batrachian reappeared a few minutes later.

"Boys and girls," he said. "I promissssse you, there is no longer anything to fear from the alligator."

Joey swallowed hard. A chilly feeling was traveling up the back of his neck. What did *that* mean? he wondered. Had his teacher stopped the alligator all by himself?

As if he had read Joey's mind, Mr. Batrachian turned to Joey and smiled slyly.

Then his eyes shone with an eerie gleam, and Joey saw a single drop of blood in the corner of his wide-stretched mouth.

Chapter

14

"**A**ll right, boys and girls," Mr. Batrachian said, smiling at the group of children clustered around him. "Now that we've all finished our lunches, it's time for you to begin looking for the objects on your assssssignment sheets."

Joey narrowed his eyes and studied his teacher's face again. He looked like a man in some ways, but in other ways he didn't. His eyes bugged out too far. His mouth was too wide, and his tongue never seemed to be still. What was he? Where had he come from?

Joey couldn't stop remembering the sight of Mr. Batrachian tearing a raccoon limb from limb and devouring it. And then going after a rampaging alligator. And maybe eating it, too. How could the man act so calm—as if nothing out of the ordinary had happened?

What was the matter with Nate and Molly? he wondered. Why couldn't they see Mr. Batrachian the way he could? How could they and the rest of the class just accept him as the new teacher? How could Nate and Molly have forgotten the night of the hurricane and the monster that had crawled out of the swamp?

He got to his feet, pulled the soggy paper out of the pocket of his wet jeans, and pretended to study it while he tried to figure out what was going on. His hands fumbled as he opened the sheet. Every nerve in his body was screaming with fear.

If the teacher *was* the thing from the swamp, then Joey's theory about the monster they had seen was probably right. Mr. Batrachian was that monster—a mutation that had been caused by the hurricane. The more he thought about it, the more Joey was convinced he was right. He was neither a science brain like Molly nor a nature nut like Nate, but he could still figure out a few things. Like maybe the stuff that had blown in from Africa had fallen on the Everglades and mixed in with the gunk in the swamp. And then

91

maybe a lightning bolt had struck the mess and caused a chemical reaction that changed things.

Molly and Nate had laughed when he said that before, but all he had to do was look at Mr. Batrachian and remember him snarling and tearing at the raccoon's carcass to know it wasn't such a far-out theory after all.

"Hey, Nate. Come here a sec," Joey called. "You, too, Molly."

Molly looked annoyed. "I have to find a bald eagle," she snapped.

"Yeah, and I've got to find a fiddler crab," said Nate. "Have you ever seen one of those things? They've got one humongous claw that they hold up in front of their bodies like a fiddle. Fiddler crabs are cool!"

"I've got to talk to you two right now!" Joey insisted. "It's important!" He tugged at Nate's sleeve angrily. "Come on."

"Okay, okay," said Nate, giving him a puzzled frown. "But make it fast."

Molly had disappeared, so Joey concentrated on Nate. "Listen, remember the thing with the bloody mouth the night of the storm? And the brown slimy thing hanging out of the Dumpster the next morning?"

Nate nodded.

"Well, I just saw it again. I *swear it!*" Joey said, raising his right hand.

"Yeah?" Nate asked uncertainly. "I thought you said it was an alligator."

"It was. I mean, I saw an alligator, too. But the other thing—the monster thing—that's what I'm talking about. I saw it back in the swamp. It was eating a dead raccoon. You've got to believe me, Nate. I'm telling the truth."

Nate squinted and looked at Joey suspiciously. "Are you sure?" he said, just above a whisper.

Joey swallowed hard and nodded. He looked around to make sure Mr. Batrachian was out of hearing range and said, "It was our teacher. He was squatting down close to the ground, gnawing on the bones and spitting out fur. Don't you see, Nate? Mr. Batrachian's not a real teacher. I don't think he's even human. He's a mutation—caused by the hurricane. *He's* the thing from the swamp!"

Nate stared at Joey as if he was trying to comprehend what his friend had just said.

Joey held his breath. If Nate didn't believe him, nobody would. And if Mr. Batrachian went from eating flies to devouring raccoons, to maybe even eating alligators, what would be next? Joey knew he had to figure out a way to stop him, but he couldn't do it alone.

"Powers, I agree with Molly," Nate finally said, slowly shaking his head. "You've been watching too many cartoons. You're loony tunes."

"Nate! You saw it yourself!" Joey persisted. "How can you say you didn't?"

"Yeah, well, maybe I don't want to think about that anymore. It's all over, and everything's okay now. Maybe I just want it to stay that way," said Nate.

"Maybe, *nothing*!" Joey snapped angrily. "You know what I think? I think you're a big fat chicken!" He hopped around in circles, flapping his arms like wings and making wild clucking sounds.

Nate's face got red, and he looked like he was about to explode. Doubling his fist, he lunged for Joey and yelled, "Okay, Powers—"

Suddenly the teacher stepped between them. He grabbed each boy by the shoulder and held them apart. His bulging eyes looked deep into Joey's, and his tongue flicked across his mouth as if he was licking his lips in delicious anticipation.

It felt as though a cold hand clutched Joey's heart.

"What's going on here?" the teacher demanded. "I won't allow fighting."

"We weren't fighting," Joey assured him hurriedly. "We were just fooling around, weren't we, Nate?"

Nate's chin was quivering as he stared into Mr. Batrachian's eyes. "Ye-yeah, that's all. We were goofing off."

Mr. Batrachian slowly let them loose. "All right. I'll believe you this time, but it had better not happen again," he warned. "Hurry along now, boys. We don't have all day, you know, and we'll have to go deeper into the swamp if you don't find thingssssss around here."

His eyes took on a glow of anticipation that made Joey shiver.

Deeper into the swamp? No way! he thought. Is that what he really wants? To lure us back where no one could ever find us?

Joey looked around frantically, searching for a stand of cypress trees. That was where he would find a strangler fig. If he could find it, then maybe he could help Nate find his fiddler crab, and they could all go back to Ochopee where it was safe.

Suddenly Joey caught a glimpse of dark clouds spreading across the sun and casting long shadows on the floor of the swamp.

Other kids had noticed, too. They rushed up to the teacher, calling, "Mr. Batrachian, it's going to rain. We'd better go home now."

"Nonsensssssse," he replied, waving them away with a hand. "Get on with your assignments."

Before Joey could respond, jagged lightning stabbed the ground just a few feet away, thunder rolled across the sky, and the smell of ozone filled the air. He looked up just as a fat drop of rain splattered into his eye.

"Hey, let's get out of here! It's gonna storm!" he shouted gleefully. Maybe the rain would save them!

He saw Nate open his mouth to yell something, too, but the sound was lost in the next crash of thunder. Then the sky opened up, and rain poured down in torrents.

Instantly the water level in the swamp began to rise until it was up to Joey's ankles.

"Mr. Batrachian!" he shouted. "Let's *go!*"

Now everyone was yelling at him.

"Mr. Batrachian!"

"Mr. Batrachian!"

The teacher scowled. "All right! All right! Have it your way! Run back to school like a bunch of sissies, but we'll be back!" he said. His voice was low and sinister. "*I promissssssse you,* we'll be back tomorrow!"

The class dashed through the rain. Joey

turned to run back to the school, also, smacking into Nate, who was standing still and staring openmouthed at something over Joey's shoulder.

Joey swallowed hard. He was almost afraid to look around, but he had to. It was Mr. Batrachian. The teacher hadn't followed the class. Instead he was standing with his face upturned into the rain as if he were in a trance. Rain streamed into his wide-open eyes. He was taking in deep gulps of water and smiling as he licked his lips with his long ropelike tongue.

"*Sheese!* Look at that!" whispered Nate. He grabbed Joey's arm in terror. "He *is* the thing from the swamp! Let's get out of here!"

Without looking back, the boys took off at a run.

Chapter 15

Joey could barely drag himself out of bed the next morning. He had spent the night filled with terror, thinking about Mr. Batrachian until his head ached. He was still convinced that he was right about the teacher. What did he want? And where had he gotten such a weird name? Joey had never heard it before.

He had tried to talk to Nate again after school, but Nate had refused to listen. Joey could tell that he was scared. He was more than scared. He was terrified. But did Nate think that if he ignored what had happened, Mr. Batrachian would just go away?

"Forget it, Powers, before I punch your lights out," Nate had said in a trembling voice.

After supper Joey had called Molly. If he couldn't make Nate face up to the truth, maybe he could convince her. After all, she was the smartest kid in the class.

At first there had been only silence on the line after Joey told her what he and Nate had seen. When she spoke, her voice had been filled with uncertainty. "I don't know, Joey. I want to believe you. I mean, I know what we saw during the storm—or thought we saw, but—"

"But what? I'm telling you the truth," Joey had insisted. "And think about how he looks. You can't tell me you really think he looks normal."

"I know," she had said. "He does look weird. And I can't stand the way he's always licking his lips. But it's impossible! It's not scientific! There is no such thing as a mutant. And besides, even if it were possible—and I'm not saying I think it is—what does he want? Why did he come to our school?"

"I don't know," Joey had admitted. "But Mr. Batrachian's here for a reason, and it's not because he likes kids."

Now the rain was gone, and morning light was streaming in through his bedroom window. Mr. Batrachian had promised the class that today they would go back into the swamp. Joey shuddered at the thought.

The face that looked back at him from the bathroom mirror was a wreck. Bloodshot eyes. Messy hair. And a sour expression.

Suddenly an idea hit him like a thunderbolt. He looked back in the mirror and grinned.

I look sick, he thought. All I have to do is convince Mom that I *am* sick, and she'll let me stay home from school today!

The idea made him dizzy with relief. No Mr. Batrachian looking at him with those sinister bulging eyes. No flycatcher tongue, darting in and out of the wide mouth. No blood and gore at lunchtime. And best of all, no worry that Mr. Batrachian would lure him deep into the swamp and hurt him.

He thought a minute. The first thing his mother always did when he complained that he was sick was to feel his face and forehead to see if he had fever. He slapped his hand on his face. It was cool.

At the same instant, he spotted her hair dryer sitting in its holder by the sink. He grabbed it, turned the settings to HOT and HIGH, and flipped on the switch. A blazing blast of air roared across his face, taking away his breath. He held the blow-dryer there until his cheeks felt warm.

He glanced at his watch. The timing was perfect. She would be leaving for work in exactly three minutes. His dad had left ten minutes earlier.

Joey opened the bathroom door and called down the hall in the most forlorn voice he could muster. "Mom! I don't feel good!"

It worked. Five minutes later he was tucked back in bed, kissed on the forehead, and promised that she would call him every hour from work to see how he was. It was all he could do to keep the sick look on his face and not laugh out loud.

But the relief he had felt at first didn't last long. He climbed out of bed and paced back and forth in his room. The questions that had deviled him all night were still there, along with some new ones.

What was Mr. Batrachian doing right now? he wondered when his watch said it was time for class to begin. And what did he want with their class? He had to have a reason for being at their school.

They must be heading for the swamp now, he thought a few minutes later. A vision of Nate, Molly, and his other schoolmates following the teacher into the eerie Everglades popped into his mind.

Were they in danger? Was he home safe in bed while Mr. Batrachian was luring his friends into the swamp for who knows what?

He looked around his comfortable room as guilt flooded his mind. Was he a chicken, after all? Maybe he should check things out and see what the teacher was up to. Maybe he should sneak back to the spot they had gone to yesterday. Of course there was nothing he could do if he found them. He wasn't a hero who could jump out from behind a mangrove and stop Mr. Batrachian from doing something awful.

Still, he thought, he had to find out what was going on. He had to know if his friends were in danger.

He threw on his clothes, stopping in the kitchen only long enough to make a couple of peanut butter-and-jelly sandwiches, which he stuffed into his pockets. Then he ran out of the house.

The streets of Ochopee were almost empty. The kids were all in school. Adults were at work. He heard only the low drone of mosquitoes in the hot morning air as he jogged toward the swamp.

His heart pounded. Would he be able to pick up their trail and sneak up on the class without being seen? And what if he did and saw something awful? What would he do then?

Joey rounded a corner and glanced toward the school building on his right. The doors were all closed. The playground was empty.

A new thought hit him. What if Mr. Batrachian had changed his mind about taking the class back into the swamp today? It was a cloudy day. Maybe the teacher thought it might rain again and changed his mind about the field trip. What if they were all in school, and he went into the swamp alone and got lost? He might never be found. Or worse, he might get eaten by an alligator—or be mauled by a bear.

"I'd better make sure they're gone," he murmured to himself.

Joey looked around to make sure no one saw him; then he ducked low and skittered across the playground. His breathing turned to nervous panting as he flattened himself against the building and slid along the wall toward one of the windows of his classroom.

He raised his head so that his eyes were even with the windowsill and peered through the glass. Empty. The classroom was deserted. He swallowed hard.

That meant Mr. Batrachian had done it. He had taken the class into the swamp just like he had promised. I have to go find them, Joey thought. *I have to!*

He started to turn away when something on Mr. Batrachian's desk caught his eye. It was the book the teacher read all the time when the class was doing silent reading. Joey thought it was probably a child psychology book because the last word in the title was *CHILDREN.*

He squinted at the title. Maybe now he could see the whole thing. But the way the sun was slanting across the desk made it impossible. Only the word *CHILDREN* was readable.

"Who cares?" he mumbled. But something kept him from turning away. Suddenly he had to know what that book was about. If Mr. Batrachian was a mutation, as Joey suspected, what was so special about that book?

Joey looked around the silent school yard. There was still no one in sight. Cautiously he raised the window and hoisted himself up, dropping into the room with a soft thud.

He tiptoed across the room to the desk and looked down at the book. He could see the whole title now, and he sighed with disappointment. There was nothing weird or mysterious about the title. It said:

PREPARING CHILDREN

"Like I thought. Just a crummy child psychology book on teaching kids about life and growing up and stuff," Joey muttered. He started to leave and then stopped. He couldn't help glancing at the book again. It didn't look like a psychology book—at least not what he thought one would look like. This book was thin and small, and it had rings in it like a binder and tabs along the sides of the pages.

He walked over to the desk, set the book on its spine, and let it fall open. The pages parted, and he stared down with horror at what was written there.

Roast Child with Mushroom and Walnut Stuffing

Joey gasped.
PREPARING CHILDREN was a cookbook!

Chapter

16

Joey ran a trembling finger down the list of ingredients.

1 plump child, approximately 85 lbs.
10 lbs. wild mushrooms, thinly sliced
10 lbs. walnuts, chopped
5 lbs. butter, melted
20 cups bread crumbs
1 cup each fresh-snipped sage and thyme
salt and pepper to taste

He gulped and read on.

Rinse child under cold running water. Dry well with paper towels.
Preheat oven to 325° F.

Joey couldn't stand to read any further. He swept the book onto the floor and spun around, staring into space.

Shaking with fright, he stood in the empty classroom. It was too horrible to be true. But it was! Now he understood why Mr. Batrachian had come to their school. He was hungry! And he had been reading a cookbook right in front of the class and licking his lips in anticipation of a delicious meal made of a boy or a girl.

Right now he was probably luring his victims into the swamp! They'd be helpless and under his power there!

Joey raced toward the window. There was no use calling his parents or even the police. They hadn't believed him before when he and Nate and Molly had told them about the monster. Why would they believe him now? They'd probably say the cookbook was some kind of joke. No, he knew what he had to do. He had to find his class and try to stop Mr. Batrachian himself.

He grabbed the cookbook and stuck it under his shirt. Then he dove out the window and hit the ground running. Molly and Nate would believe him when they saw the book—if it wasn't too late!

The spot where the class had entered the

swamp yesterday was only a couple of blocks away. He prayed they went in at in the same place today. His feet pounded the ground as he raced for it.

The clouds had disappeared. Stepping out of the bright morning sunlight and into the musty twilight of the swamp was like entering another world—a deadly, dangerous world. Joey shivered and peered around. Had there been other mutations caused by the storm? Were there other creatures like his teacher, lurking in the shadows? Hungry mutations watching him move deeper into the gloom? Falling in behind him? Waiting to pounce and drag him below the surface of the dark water?

Somewhere in the distance a bird squalled. Joey jumped. It had sounded like a bird. But was it? Or was it a child? Someone in his class, crying out for help? Maybe Molly or Nate?

He looked around desperately for footprints in the mud. They weren't hard to find. They led off through the dense mangrove forest.

He cupped his hands around his mouth and shouted, "Nate! Molly! Anybody! Where are you?"

Sweat popped out on his forehead as he started running again. It was 10:35, already the middle of the morning. How soon would the kids start getting hungry and beg the teacher to stop for lunch?

How soon would Mr. Batrachian get hungry?

"Hello!" he shouted as loudly as he could. "Can anyone hear me? Nate! Molly! Where are you?"

"*I* can hear you, Joey Powerssssss," said a deep voice behind him.

Joey froze in his tracks. His heart jumped into his throat as he spun around. Mr. Batrachian was standing before him, licking his lips with his long, pointed tongue.

"Um, I'm sorry I'm late," Joey began. The words rushed out in a breathy whisper. "I . . . I overslept . . . and when I got . . . got to school . . . um, you had already left."

A smile stretched slowly across the teacher's face.

"Is that sssssso?"

"Um, yeah, and I guess I'd . . . I'd better hurry and catch up with the class." Joey's knees were turning to rubber and he was afraid he'd collapse right there at the teacher's feet.

He's not a teacher! Joey reminded himself. *He's a mutant! And he wants to eat children!*

"Which way did everybody go?" he managed to whisper.

Suddenly there was a rustling in the bushes, and Molly broke through into the clearing. Her eyes were wide, and she had a frantic look on her face.

"Mr. Batrachian! Come quickly!" she pleaded. "We can't find Nate. He's disappeared!"

She had barely gotten the words out when Todd Dooley rushed up. "Something's happened to Nate! He's gone!" he said breathlessly.

A look of irritation passed over Mr. Batrachian's face. "Nonsense," he snapped, and stomped off in the direction Molly and Todd had come from. "I saw Nate just a few minutes ago. He's fine. Come now and get back to work on your assignments."

Joey stumbled along after the others. Catching up with Molly, he asked, "What happened?"

"We were just doing what Mr. Batrachian said to do," Molly said anxiously. "We were all fanned out looking for wild mushrooms. Nate was there one minute and gone the next. He just vanished!"

Joey gulped. "Molly! Did you say that you were looking for wild *mushrooms*?" he demanded.

She threw him an angry look. "So what? The

only thing that's important is that Nate's missing in the swamp."

Joey's mind was racing. Was it an accident that *PREPARING CHILDREN* had fallen open to the recipe for Roast Child with Mushroom and Walnut Stuffing?

"Molly, I can prove that what I said about Mr. Batrachian is true," Joey said hurriedly. "Look at this," he said, reaching inside his shirt and pulling out a small book. "It's the book he's always reading. It's called *PREPARING CHILDREN* and it's a cookbook!"

Molly stopped in her tracks and stared at the book. Slowly Joey let it fall open to the recipe for Roast Child with Mushroom and Walnut Stuffing.

Molly gasped. "And we were hunting mushrooms! Oh, Joey, you don't think . . ."

Joey knew he didn't have to answer. The expression on Molly's face told him that she was finally convinced.

"I've got something to show you too," she said, Taking a piece of paper out of her pocket. "After you called last night, I started thinking about what a weird name Batrachian is. I went to the dictionary and looked it up. Wait till you see what it means."

Joey looked down at the paper and held his breath.

ba•tra•chi•an. *adj.* pertaining to animals of the order *Batrachia.*

Ba•tra•chia. *n.*, pl. **1.** an order of amphibians without tails, including frogs and toads. **2.** loosely, all amphibians.

Joey's heart pounded wildly. Now he knew the truth. All of it. Mr. Batrachian had warty skin, slick brown hair, and he wore a brown leather suit. Most frogs were green, but toads were brown. *Mr. Batrachian was a mutant toad.*

A huge, hungry toad who was getting hungrier by the minute! Yesterday morning he had sucked a fly out of the air and eaten it. At noon in the swamp it had taken a raccoon to satisfy him—and he'd probably devoured an alligator, too.

The hair on the back of Joey's neck stood up. What was he going to eat today?

Chapter

17

Suddenly Joey heard it again—the eerie sound of a bird crying in the swamp. But was it a bird?

"Did you hear that?" he whispered.

She nodded. Her eyes were filled with alarm.

"What do you think it was?" she asked nervously. "It sounded—"

"Yeah, I know. More like a human than a bird," he said.

Joey shot a quick look down the path. Mr. Batrachian and Todd were out of sight.

"It could be Nate," Joey said solemnly.

He swallowed nervously and slowly looked around at the dark, spooky swamp surrounding them. Ghostly mangrove trees stood silently with

113

their roots outstretched like tiptoeing feet. Not far away an alligator floated in the water, only the triangle of its bulging eyes and nostrils visible above the water. Creepy, crawly things were everywhere. Taking a deep breath, he said, "We've got to find him on our own."

Molly nodded. "Okay," she said seriously. "Let's go."

"I think the sound we heard came from that direction," said Joey.

He took a step forward and stopped. It was the darkest part of the swamp, where the roots of the mangroves formed a thick wall and the cypress trees blotted out the sunshine. Water lapping against the trees and the hum of insects were the only sounds. Joey could hardly breathe for the stench of decay and the odor of rotting vegetation.

"Maybe we should get help," Molly offered timidly.

"Who would believe us?" Joey grumbled. He didn't wait for an answer. Instead he slogged off through the ankle-deep water, pushing aside branches and grabbing mangrove roots to help him stay on his feet.

Molly hurried to catch up with him. "Nate!" she called. "Nate, can you hear us?"

"Nate, where are you?" Joey yelled. "We're coming to get you."

They stopped and listened, their hearts pounding, but there was no reply.

"Come on. We've *got* to keep looking," said Joey.

Suddenly Molly screamed and pointed to a slimy creature slithering under a leaf. "That lizard! It crawled over my foot!" she cried breathlessly.

Joey took Molly's hand. "Let's stick together," he said, scanning the muck they were walking through. He didn't like lizards any better than Molly did.

They pushed their way through thick brambles that scratched their arms and faces. The deep mud sucked at their feet, making each step they took difficult.

"Nate! Where *are* you?" Molly shouted again.

"Hey, Dolinsky! What's the matter? Too chicken to show your face?" yelled Joey.

Molly gave him a furious look and opened her mouth to say something, so he quickly explained, "It's a game we play. We try to see who's the bravest. Nate'll understand . . . if he hears me."

"Shhhh," said Molly, grabbing Joey's arm. "I thought I heard something."

They strained to listen, but all they heard was silence.

Suddenly Joey sniffed the air. "Smoke!" he shouted.

"I smell it, too!" cried Molly. "But wait. Don't panic. It could mean that there are park rangers around burning off undergrowth. Park rangers could help us find Nate."

"Yeah, or it could be a fire set by all that lightning yesterday," Joey reminded her. "And you know what that could mean—flash fires that can roar over acres of trees in the blink of an eye."

Molly nodded and screamed even louder for Nate.

"Let's yell together," suggested Joey. "On the count of three. One. Two. Three."

"NATE!"

Still the swamp was silent. And the smell of smoke was getting stronger.

"What are we going to do?" Joey asked desperately. "We can't just leave him, but I'm getting scared. We could be surrounded by fire!"

Molly sniffed the air again. "I don't think so," she said slowly. "It smells more like a campfire to me. Let's look for five more minutes. If we don't find him by then, we'll have to turn back."

"Okay," Joey said anxiously. "Five more minutes."

Cautiously they made their way forward, pushing aside branches and pulling one foot after another out of the muck.

Suddenly a terrible thought popped into Joey's mind. "Uh-oh, Molly. We forgot something. Something important."

"What?" she asked.

"We didn't mark our trail. How will we ever find our way out of here?"

They looked back over their shoulders. The way they had come was blocked by walking roots and brambles. They looked in every direction, but everything appeared the same. It was as if the swamp had closed around them, swallowing them up. Burying them in a watery tomb.

"Oh, my gosh!" said Molly, her voice trembling. "We're lost, and no one will ever find us. We'll probably die in here!"

"Come on," said Joey, trying to sound braver than he felt. "We said we'd look for Nate for five more minutes. We have three to go. Then we'll worry about finding our way out of here."

Joey stomped on, pulling Molly along behind him.

Suddenly he stepped onto firm ground in a clearing and sucked in his breath. He felt Molly stiffen. She saw it, too.

They stood in terrified silence. A small fire was burning in the center of the clearing. Mr. Batrachian was squatting, hunched over it, his back to them. He was feeding sticks into the flames.

Nearby, Nate's body slumped against ropes that tied him to a tree.

His eyes were closed.

He was as still as death.

Chapter

Slowly Mr. Batrachian looked around, as if he had felt the stares of their horror-filled eyes on his back. A smile spread across his toadlike face. His bulging eyes gleamed with satisfaction.

"Oh, how wonderful!" he said, rubbing his hands together in anticipation. "Now I won't merely have a meal, I'll have a *three-courssssssse banquet!*" He threw back his head and laughed. The sound rolled over them and echoed through the mangroves like the deep roar of thunder.

Joey tried to back away, but his legs were frozen to the spot. He stared at the mutant's huge round body as it rose from the ground. The creature's tongue licked out in quick darts and his neck throbbed.

Suddenly he lunged for them in one gigantic hop. His tongue shot toward them like a whip.

"You can't get away from me. Don't even try," he warned. "Thissssss is *my* swamp. *My* home. And I have the power to rule it and everything in it—including *you two!*"

"You really are a mutant!" Molly shouted as she ducked away from him.

The giant toad hopped again and landed where she had been an instant before. He gave her a sly grin. "Ah, yes. You've discovered my secret," he said. His eyes bulged, and his tongue darted out and grabbed a dragonfly out of the air. With a great sigh of satisfaction he gulped and went on. "I was once just a lowly toad. But when the hurricane blew through the Everglades, something wonderful happened. I began to change. To grow! To know things I had never known before! And to develop an *enormous* appetite! I kept on growing and kept on changing until I became what you see before you. A respected sssssschoolteacher," he said, and laughed again.

"What . . . what happened to Mr. Vernon?" Joey asked, afraid of the answer.

The monster chuckled. "Can't you guessssss? Ah! What a delicious memory." He licked his lips with his gigantic tongue. "But I've developed a taste for gourmet food ever since I found a wonderful book," he said slyly. "It's called PREPARING CHILDREN. But I see you've already found it," he added, nodding toward the book in Joey's hand.

"You bet I found it! But that's not all. I figured you out a long time ago!" shouted Joey. "You're the thing from the swamp!"

"If you know so much about me, then you know what fate is in store for you," the toad said with a sinister sneer. "It's really no different from you humans eating hamburgers, pork chops, or"—his face took on a ghastly look—"*frog legs!*"

"Come on, Joey! Run!" screamed Molly as the giant mutant started toward them again.

"We can't leave Nate!" Joey shouted. He could see his friend starting to stir, as if he were coming out of a deep sleep.

Suddenly Batrachian's tongue snapped over Joey's head like a crackling electrical power line.

"Don't let it touch you or you're dead!" shouted Molly. "That's how toads catch their prey!"

Joey ignored her. He had thought of a plan. He thumbed his nose and made a face at the giant toad as he began backing toward the edge of the clearing.

"Come on, slimeball. Come and get me," he urged.

Batrachian took a great hop in Joey's direction. His tongue flicked forward like that of a striking snake.

"That's right, swamp breath," Joey coaxed. "You've got the moves. Just keep 'em coming this way."

Out of the side of his mouth, Joey called to Molly. "Hurry, untie Nate!"

Ducking and weaving like a boxer, Joey dodged the mutant toad's deadly lashing tongue.

"I'll get you, you miserable brat," Batrachian said with a snarl. "Call me a sssssslimeball, will you? I'll grind you into ssssssausage!"

While the monster talked, Joey dug into the pockets of his jeans. He carefully opened the lock-top sandwich bags and pulled out a peanut butter-and-jelly sandwich with each hand. He smiled to himself, remembering that he had spread the peanut butter extra thick in case his trip to the swamp made him hungrier than usual.

Holding them high in the air, he took careful aim at the toad's wide-open mouth.

"Fire one!" he shouted, heaving the first sandwich into the giant mutant's mouth. "Fire two! Bull's-eye! Bull's-eye!" he cried.

Batrachian froze. He looked at Joey in astonishment for an instant and then worked his jaws, trying desperately to spit out the sticky mess that filled his mouth like cement and coated his tongue, trapping it inside.

"Hurry, Molly!" cried Joey. "This won't stop him for long."

Nate was awake now, and he and Molly both tugged at the knots, frantically trying to get him free.

Batrachian roared like a wounded lion, scooping the peanut butter and jelly out of his mouth and off his tongue.

"Come on! Let's get out of here!" shouted Molly as the last of the ropes holding Nate fell away.

All three took off at a run, scrambling through brambles and bounding over bushes.

The monster crashed through the underbrush after them.

"Come back here, you miserable children!" he shouted. "You insufferable brats! When I get my hands on you, I'm going to boil you until your eyessssss pop out!"

"Faster!" urged Joey. "He's gaining on us!"

"I'm going to slice you and dice you and mince you!" the mutant screamed. "And cook you in hot oil!"

123

Suddenly Joey found himself in another clearing and skidded to a stop at the edge of a dark lake. Molly and Nate stopped beside him. They looked in horror at the dozens of alligators floating in a ring around the shoreline in front of them.

Instantly Batrachian came out of the jungle behind them, his long tongue free and lashing the air like a whip.

"Oh, no!" Molly sobbed. Tears filled her eyes. *"We're trapped!"*

Chapter

Suddenly the swamp grew deadly still. Songbirds stopped calling. Insects stopped buzzing. The lapping water became motionless. Even the breeze stirring the leaves became calm.

"What's happening?" Molly whispered, clutching Joey's arm.

Batrachian stopped in his tracks. He looked around in horror, as if he could hear sounds the children couldn't hear. Jerking his head from side to side in a frenzy, he darted in first one direction and then another.

Suddenly, out of the corner of his eye, Joey thought he saw something move. He blinked and looked around, but everything was still. The next instant another movement caught his eye. And then another.

Staring in fascination, he watched the outstretched root of a nearby mangrove tree reach to the ground like a foot stepping down. Then the root on another tree did the same. And another.

"Look!" cried Nate, his mouth hanging open in awe. "The walking trees! They're really *walking*!"

Before their astonished eyes the ancient mangrove trees began to close in around Batrachian.

"No! No!" The mutant backed away in horror, shoving at the trees and trying to fight off the walking roots. But there was nowhere to go.

Joey's scalp tingled as he watched the trees slowly march on, encircling the struggling, gasping monster. He flailed his arms, trying to fend them off. But on they moved—pressing in on him, smothering him—until Batrachian was completely surrounded and hidden from view.

Joey slowly shook his head. "I don't believe it," he whispered in awe. "But it makes sense."

"What makes sense?" asked Molly.

"That Batrachian wouldn't be the only mutation in the whole storm," Joey replied, still shaking his head in wonder. "The walking trees. How else could they move like that?"

"Oh, no!" cried Nate. "I refuse to believe this! It can't be happening!"

"You're right," said Molly. "It's *impossible!*"

Joey pointed to a snakelike vine slithering across the ground.

"It's a strangler fig," he said. "Just like the one on my assignment sheet. It's got to be another mutation."

He stared in amazement as the vine slithered its way through the tangle of walking trees and disappeared into the center.

An instant later a bloodcurdling scream filled the air.

The children clutched each other in terror as the echo of the scream faded and the swamp fell silent again. Moment after moment went by. Not a leaf stirred. Not an insect hummed. The only sound was the thudding of their hearts.

Then Joey felt a slight breeze. He heard the hum of bugs start up. A butterfly floated in the direction of the newly formed mangrove forest standing before them. An occasional leaf stirred, but the roots stayed firmly planted where they were. The walking trees had stopped walking.

"I guess it's over," Molly said softly.

Joey nodded. "It's sort of like nature has put itself back in balance. A couple of good mutations got rid of a bad mutation to make things normal again. And it'll be our secret forever."

"Right," said Nate. "Nobody would ever believe us anyway if we told them about a giant mutant toad with an appetite for kids."

"Or walking trees that really walked," added Molly. "Or strangler figs that strangled something besides trees."

"I'm really glad old Batrachian got what was coming to him," said Nate.

Joey glanced toward the new mangrove forest and broke into a smile. "He certainly did get what was coming to him," he said gleefully. "Look at that."

An ancient alligator was lumbering out of the mangrove thicket and heading for the lake. It stopped and glanced at Joey, Nate, and Molly, baring its teeth in a sinister grin.

A single drop of blood glistened at the corner of its mouth.

The Everglades had returned to normal. The last remnants of the hurricane were gone. The great swamp had settled back to the way it had always been.

About the Author

Betsy Haynes has written over fifty books for children, including *The Great Mom Swap,* the bestselling The Fabulous Five series, and the Taffy Sinclair books. *Taffy Goes to Hollywood* received the Phantom's Choice Award for Best Juvenile Series Book of 1990.

When she isn't writing, Betsy loves to travel, and she and her husband, Jim, spend as much time as possible aboard their boat, *Nut & Honey.* Betsy and her husband live on Marco Island, Florida, and have two grown children, two dogs, and a black cat with extra toes.